CARMEN

CARMEN

JOHN BENTON

John Benton Books
Box 94304
218 So. Madison
Pasadena, CA 91109

Scripture quotations in this volume are from the *King James Version of the Bible.*

ISBN 0-8007-8159-7

Library of Congress Catalog Card Number:74-112463
Printed in the United States of America

To
Mr. and Mrs. Walter Hoving
who have helped to make new lives possible
for all Carmens

Introduction

AS YOU READ THIS story, you may find it unbelievable—things like this don't really happen. But the events related here *did* happen, and *do* happen, every day, to girls who come to our Home.

Before I wrote each chapter I interviewed our girls, in order to have their stories fresh in my mind. The result is a composite of the stories they told me—stories of addiction, prostitution, perversion, and worse.

But it is also a story of forgiveness—the forgiveness of Christ. No matter how far a girl may plunge into the depths of sin, she can know that her past is forgiven in Christ, and that Christ will give her His strength for the present, and His faith for the future. All she need do is ask.

JOHN BENTON

Prologue

WAVES OF NAUSEA wakened me. I barely made it to the bathroom. When I came out, I looked at the clock—7:15 P.M. Vinnie was still asleep, so I figured I might as well get started on the night's work.

I got dressed quickly and went out onto the dark and nearly deserted street. I pulled my collar up against the raw, sleety wind and sauntered along, searching for a man—any man—who'd kick in the bucks to get Vinnie and me a fix.

Fifteen minutes later, I was still eyeing every man who walked by, cursing each one under my breath. I knew I had the goods: five-foot-two, 36-20-34; long, curling brown hair; eyes with lashes long enough to bat, and a smile that could melt any man, if only he'd look. Where was he?

A gust nearly blew me off my feet. I ducked into a doorway to catch my breath, and tried desperately to focus my thoughts on something—anything—that would get my mind off the drug my body screamed for. Scraps of this and that skittered around in my weary brain: a flash from my old days in New Jersey, when I was a child; another of Vinnie and me shooting up our last bag last night.

I wiped my runny nose and looked hopefully up the street—not a soul in sight.

What in the world was I doing here? How had I gotten here and become nothing but a sick, dirty, broken-down drug addict?

Like one in a dream, I grabbed at the flashing thoughts —at the never-never land I had lived in, before I had to stand on this street corner waiting for a pickup. The time I. . . .

CARMEN

CHAPTER • 1

It was ten o'clock and I was getting ready for bed, when I heard the front door slam. It was Dad, home at last. As I started down the hall to the bathroom, I heard Mom say, "What's the matter? You look beat."

There was no answer, but I heard footsteps going into the kitchen and the refrigerator door slam, so I kept on going. After I brushed my teeth and washed up, I started back to my room, then hesitated and backtracked the few steps to the living room door. I glanced in and saw Dad sitting on the sofa. He was all hunched over, just staring at the floor; one hand held a half-eaten sandwich, the other an untouched glass of milk. Mom was nowhere to be seen. My heart went out to him. He looked so lonely and so sad —whatever could be the matter?

I crept over to the sofa quietly, perched on the arm, put my hand on his shoulder, and asked in a gentle voice, "Dad, what's the trouble?"

I waited for an answer, but Dad gave no sign of hearing; he continued to stare at the floor. I tried to put my arm around him, but he jerked free so fast half of the milk spilled onto the rug. Then he turned on me. His eyes, red from crying, glared with a hatred I had never seen in anyone before—hatred for me, Mom, the world, anyone who tried to help him.

"Get to bed!" he snarled. "This is none of your business."

"But, Dad. . . ." I protested and he gave me a wild shove.

"Get outta here, before you're sorry."

I didn't wait. I was scared, but I was hurt too—why wouldn't he let me help him? I ran into my room, slammed the door and threw myself across the bed. A lump started to grow in my throat, and a few tears trickled down my cheeks. It's great when parents share their happiness with you, but shouldn't they share their sorrows too? It doesn't seem fair to leave a kid out—after all, I wasn't such a kid. I was fourteen. They say that when two people get married they're supposed to share their happiness and sorrow together—why not with their children? Seems to me, they'd all wind up closer together. A home isn't just a house or a building; it should be a place where there is love and concern for all and by all, for happiness *and* sorrow.

The lump wouldn't go away; it grew bigger and the trickle of tears grew into a torrent. I sobbed until I could cry no more. Then, mercifully, I fell asleep.

But not for long. My throat was sore and dry; my swollen eyelids ached as I forced them open. Gradually, my eyes focused on the room around me—a really pretty room which you might call a typical teen-ager's room. They wandered from the ruffled vanity to the bulletin board, from the matching curtains to the record player, finally to the canopy over my head. (For once, the room was neat —just this morning Mom had nagged me to "Clean it up or else!")

I thought of the clothes in the closet. It's really a crazy

world! How could I be lying here in a beautiful room like this, with most of the things a teen-ager wants, and be so miserable and unhappy? Why was my home such a hell?

The trouble really started after we bought our new home in New Jersey. Sure, Dad was an alcoholic before we moved here; he was a first-class phony, too, but he never actually got violent before we lived here—never hit me or Mom. Maybe it was the pressure of higher monthly payments; maybe it was all the new furniture we bought. Whatever it was, our happy home was going down the drain fast.

Our house was really beautiful, and I loved it; we all did, at first. It was a far cry from the seedy Brooklyn neighborhood we'd moved from. Maybe the old row houses there were all right once, but from as early as I can remember the whole area was pretty rundown and getting more so every day. Blistered paint peeled off the frame houses; windows were boarded up, where panes of glass were missing; others had gaping holes, with ragged slivers of glass jutting out.

Mom remembered it from better times, when middle-class Irish, Italian and German working people lived there with a few Jews thrown in for good measure. She'd been brought up right around the corner from where we lived, and she told me all the families took great pride in their tiny gardens and courts and worked hard to keep them up.

I guess her own childhood wasn't too good: both of her parents worked and were gone all day. According to her they worked *all* the time and had little to say to her or to each other.

Mom was little, like me, and kinda' plain. I guess she

wasn't too popular with the other kids and, maybe also like me, she spent a lotta time just dreaming. How else did I wind up with a romantic name like Carmen? Or was I named for one of her old neighbors? I never knew. She said she had never had many dates and, as she got older, the only fun she had was going to neighborhood dances with a couple of other girls once in a while.

It was at one of those dances that she met my dad. He was in the navy stationed at the Brooklyn Navy Yard. A buddy of his came from Mom's neighborhood and he took Dad to a dance.

Dad never talked about his parents or his home. From the little bit I learned from Mom, his home was worse than hers. He left it when he was fourteen, quit school in the eighth grade and never went back. Mom said as far as she knew he never saw any of his family after that either; she didn't even know if he had any sisters or brothers.

He knocked around for awhile after he left home—hoboed and did odd jobs here and there—and then he joined the navy.

Dad was a big man—six-foot-one and kinda' burly. He had a booming laugh, and white teeth that showed in an infectious grin. He was glib, too, always. He could charm the birds right out of the trees if he wanted to—trouble was, at home, he didn't much want to, especially if he was drinking.

When I was pretty small, I can remember both Mom and Dad going on drinking sprees. I'd wake up in the middle of the night and hear them out in the kitchen; they'd laugh a lot, but sometimes they had awful fights. Finally Mom quit altogether and she tried to talk Dad into doing it, but he just shrugged and said, "Everybody's gotta have *some* vice." He kept going until he became a real alcoholic; he couldn't start the day without a drink. He wasn't a bum or anything like that; as a matter of fact, he had a good job as a used-car salesman but he just hit that bottle.

Once Mom talked him into going to Alcoholics Anonymous, but he didn't last long. Said he couldn't stand the soul-baring and that most of the guys there had worse problems than he did. *I* think he just used that as an excuse because he didn't have the guts to quit.

Dad was a grade-A phony. When he was going to AA, he even served as an elder in the church. He used to laugh and say to Mom, "They're proud of me. I'm reforming, aren't I? And the church is helping to rehabilitate me!" He was always a respected member of the community. What a laugh! If they could only have seen him cursing and drinking at home.

But all that happened before the minister started coming to our house regularly—back in Brooklyn. I was in the fifth grade then, and he used to come by every Saturday to have a Bible study. He and Dad argued all the time. One Saturday, Dad ordered him out of the house and told him never to come back. For a while the minister came on Wednesdays and talked with Mom, but one day Dad came home early—and boy, did the fur fly! That minister lit out of there but fast when Dad roared at him and told him if he ever came back he'd kill him. Far as I know, the minister never did come back, and that was the end of religion in our household.

Although neither of my parents knew love in their own families, I think they tried to think of me—sometimes. I'm pretty sure the reason they moved to New Jersey was for me: so I'd live in a better neighborhood, have a better education and a place where I could have friends, and get off the streets to play. I really can't blame them too much. Maybe if they'd had love, they'd have been able to pass it on to me. One thing I was sure of: when I had kids, they were going to have love and lots of it!

When we first moved to Jersey, we were all excited. We all really had fun. I guess we went haywire with excitement. We didn't need a new car, since Dad was in the business, but we sure bought a lot of other stuff: new rugs, a sofa, a dinette set—I don't know what all. Mom and I did my whole bedroom up new with an antique white canopied bed, dresser and vanity, and draperies, curtains and skirt to match. Dad got carried away, too, and broke down and bought me a bulletin board, a record player and some records. He even listened to some combos with me one night.

I was pretty shy with the kids at school at first, but as my room took shape, I just *had* to show it to someone, so I got up enough nerve to ask a few girls in from time to time. It wasn't long until I had a few friends and we went back and forth—Betsy, Cathy and a few others—to each other's houses. But then Dad started drinking heavily and I quit asking anybody home. I never knew what might happen.

When I started thinking about the drinking, the fogginess went out of my mind. My dreaminess and sense of hurt vanished and the familiar frustrating fury started to build up.

I swung my legs over the side of the bed and sat bolt upright, forcing myself to remember that night just a week ago—the night Mom told me, "Forget it—just forget it,

Carmen. He never meant to hurt you. He was drunk and I'll bet he's sorry already."

Sorry? Huh! I *had* tried to push it out of my mind; after all, I was only fourteen and he had been better since—not pleasant, but not abusive either. Now, I wallowed in the pleasure of reliving that night—every second, every word, every gesture.

I had been sound asleep when loud voices from the living room wakened me. Half-groggy with sleep, I lay there trying to sort out what was going on, but when I heard a crash and a scream, I leapt from my bed and tore into the hall.

"What's going on?" I yelled.

"Get back to bed and mind your own business," Dad roared back, as I careened into the living room.

Mom was half-on, half-off the sofa, with one hand up to her face. The coffee table was upset beside her. As she tried to right herself, Dad shoved her back and snarled, "Get back there and listen to me! I'm talkin' to you."

"Get your hands off her, you dirty slob," I yelled, and flung myself on him. Anyone watching would have thought it was pretty ridiculous I guess—five-foot-two, ninety-five pounds pitting herself against a burly giant. But my rage knew no bounds. The welt on Mom's cheek sent all reason out of my head. I swarmed all over him, biting, kicking, scratching, screaming all the while, "Keep your hands off her. Hit her again and I'll kill you!"

At first Dad tried to shake me off, but, as my clawing raked his back and arms and my clinging hampered his movements, he reached one arm around and grabbed my throat. As one big paw shook me like a terrier, my grip slackened and his other hand joined the one round my neck. Silently, he tightened his hands, and I could feel the breath going out of me.

"Stop it! Stop it! You'll kill her!" Mom pleaded.

Between clenched teeth, Dad said, "I intend to."

My senses reeled; everything started to go black, as I heard a bell ringing faintly. It rang again and again, and then a gulp of air rushed into my lungs. I sucked it in gratefully and slumped to the floor.

Dully, I watched Dad answer the phone—he had dropped me in order to answer it. I watched him talk and gesture as if I were watching a puppet show. Gradually, the words came through the fog. They turned my stomach—you never heard such sweetness, such pleasantness. Dad was a respected member of the community again, he was placating some customer who'd just bought a car from him.

"No trouble, no trouble at all," he kept repeating, with a smile on his face. "That's what I'm here for—to help you any time you need help, any hour of the day."

Boy, how I wished that customer could've seen what he interrupted! "That's my Pop!" I thought wearily, as Mom helped me to my feet and steered me to bed.

I started to pace the floor. By now my rage was almost as great as Dad's had been that night. How could I respect a man who wore one face for the public and quite another for his family? God knows I had tried. Once in a while I had even succeeded—when we were all working together on the house, for example. But now? For a week, I'd tried to bury and forget my hatred, and what had I gotten for it? Tonight he'd shamed and hurt me as I'd never been before. My own Dad hated me! What could I do?

Run away! The thought hit me like a bombshell. That'd show him. But where? My excitement carried me through throwing some clothes on, but then I started to get scared. I sat down on the bed again and tried to think. I knew I had to go, but where? And when? I decided I'd better wait a while and be sure *they* were asleep before I left, so I got into bed with my clothes on, and waited. It seemed like years, but finally one o'clock came. The house was silent as a tomb, so I decided to risk it.

Shoes in hand, I crept out of the room, down the hall, and out the front door. The air smelled sweet as I slipped into my shoes and scurried down the street. It smelled even sweeter after I rounded the corner and headed for the bus station. I was free at last! It felt wonderful. After a few blocks, I realized that the streets were deserted and the few cars that came by slowed as they passed me. It scared me, so I quickened my step and finally reached the haven of the bus station. Only one old man was sitting on a bench, so I decided to figure out what to do before I went to the ticket window.

I sat on a bench behind the old man and counted up the money I'd grabbed. All I had was $3.45. I sure couldn't go far on that. Then I remembered all the stories I'd read about Greenwich Village—all the kids went there. And it wasn't far, thank goodness.

"What's the fare to Manhattan and when's the next bus?" I asked the man behind the counter.

"$2.25," he said. "Last bus at 2:40."

I shoved three dollar bills at him and he stamped the ticket and slid it over. It was only a little after two, so I sat down to map out strategy.

The old man kept looking over at me. Does he know I'm

running away from home, I wondered? I turned my eyes to the posters on the wall, but I could feel him staring at me.

Then I noticed the ticket man was picking up the phone. As he dialed, he turned his back to me. My heart plunged. Was he calling my parents? The old man's unwavering stare unnerved me more. Then sanity returned and I almost laughed. How could that guy call anyone? He didn't even know my name!

The ticket man spoke briefly and hung up, never even glancing at me. Then he began to hum and to rummage through some drawers. I relaxed and tried to figure out what I'd do when I reached the Village. I knew I didn't have enough money left for a hotel room. Oh, well, I'll worry about that when I get there, I decided.

I was really beginning to enjoy myself, imagining the fun I'd have, when the front door opened and two cops walked in. They walked directly over to me.

That lousy ticket man! He'd called the police.

"Any identification on you, Miss?" one cop asked.

"No."

"How old are you?" asked the second.

"Eighteen."

"When were you born?" the first fired back.

Without stopping to think, I blurted out the right year of my birth, and I could have bitten off my tongue! The fat was really in the fire, now, I knew. What would they do? Call my folks? My father'd kill me!

"You better come along with us. It sounds as though you're fourteen, not eighteen, and no identification, either." He nodded at the other cop ominously.

"What's your name, young lady?" asked the first cop.

"I'm Officer Bradshaw and this is Officer Jenkins."

"Beverly Carr," I replied.

I had lied about my age and they had caught me. I was lying about my name and they probably suspected that, too, but they'd have a hard time checking up on *that,* I figured.

"When did you run away?" Jenkins asked.

I knew they had me cold, so I told the truth. "Tonight."

Bradshaw handed me into the back seat of the patrol car and got in beside me; Jenkins got into the driver's seat and we pulled away from the curb.

"Where are you taking me?"

"Youth House."

"Youth House," I yelled. "I'm no criminal—all I've done is run away. Just take me home, please."

"Can't do that," Jenkins snapped. "Have to turn in a report. You kids don't know this—maybe if you did, more of you'd stay home where you belong—but you can't just run off and forget about it. Somebody's legally responsible for you until you're eighteen. If your parents can't look after you, then the court has to take care of you. One way or another, someone has to look out for you."

It took about ten minutes to get to the big gray building I'd seen so many times, and another five to park and get through the front door. The cops led me through still another door—a big double one—and stopped before a desk.

"Well, what've we got here?" The guy behind the desk asked half-cynically, half-jokingly.

I didn't bother to answer; I just glared at him. What'd he expect? A horse? A rhinoceros? I was just a lousy little runaway, and a mad and scared one, too. Why'd they have to treat me like a criminal? Like a delinquent? All I'd done was run away from home. Lots of people had done that; even my own Dad, and no one had ever punished him.

The cop got up from the desk, beckoned to me, and led me into an anteroom. He sat me on a sofa and walked out. Staring at me from the opposite wall was the picture of a familiar face, the mayor. His eyes seemed to look straight through me and ask, "All right, young lady, what have you been up to?"

I shifted my eyes and wondered if he had ever run away.

I sat there and squirmed until a rough-looking woman walked in. She sat down behind the desk, looked straight into my eyes and said nothing.

I squirmed some more, until she finally asked, "What's your name?"

I knew I couldn't monkey with this dame, so I said, "Carmen."

"Carmen what?"

"Petra."

She reached into a drawer, pulled out a form and wrote for a second or two. I guess she was filling in my name.

"Address?" she snapped. Then: "Phone number? School?" and a bunch of other stuff. She wrote it all down as I answered.

"Ever been arrested?"

"Are you kidding?"

"Just answer the question, yes or no?" She didn't even look up.

"No."

She scribbled again, then rose and said, "All right, come with me."

She led me down the hall past another couple of doors and into a small side room.

"Take your clothes off and get into the shower," she ordered.

I stood there, waiting for her to leave.

"Get a move on—off with the clothes." She reached out and undid the top button of my jacket.

"Get your filthy hands off; I'll do it myself."

She grabbed me and drew me real close. Her face was only about two inches from mine.

"Listen, sweetheart," she drawled, "don't talk that way to me, or you're liable to get that pretty little face slapped. I'm the matron on duty here. Give me a bad time and you're liable to get pushed around a little. Understand?"

Only my tiptoes were touching the floor. I understood all right; she meant business, and I wasn't going to argue with her.

She relaxed her grip and I scurried out of my clothes. My face was red. Even in gym, I'd never stripped before anyone before, and the matron's eyes examined every inch of my body.

She walked over to a shower and turned it on full blast.

"Get in," she commanded.

I stuck one foot in and hesitated; the water was freezing.

"Get in!"

I felt a push from behind and jumped in. I washed as best I could; the water did warm up a little toward the end. When I stepped out of the shower, the matron examined me before she threw a towel over. After I was dry, she tossed me a pair of pajamas—institutional white, stiff and coarse.

"Pajamas?" I exclaimed. "I thought you were taking me home."

"Sorry, kiddo." She didn't sound it. "But you're staying here for awhile."

"How long?"

"Depends. Depends on your attitude; how well you do here; whether your parents want you; whether you've done something bad; whether you've got someplace to go."

"But all I want to do is go home," I wailed. How long would I *really* have to stay? Every minute seemed like an eternity.

The matron didn't answer. She opened the doors and motioned me to follow her. We went up a flight of stairs and she pulled out a bunch of keys and unlocked the door. After we stepped through it, she locked it again, then paused and double-checked the lock.

My jaw dropped; I'd never get out of this place, I knew. The matron glanced at me; I was afraid and she knew it. *And* she was enjoying it.

We walked on down the hall and finally stopped at a door. Out came the keys again and I entered a tiny cell. It had a window in the door and I noticed another small window with bars and a heavy screen outside. The only piece of furniture was a cot. The matron switched on a light and said, "You'll sleep here. Tomorrow morning we'll have a little chat."

She nodded briefly, closed and locked the door, double-checked the lock and walked off.

This was solitary confinement! I'd read and heard of places like this—but just for running away?

I started to bawl. Why in the world had I run away? So home wasn't so hot; it was certainly better than this. Finally I got hold of myself. Cut it out, I said to myself. That's what that dame wants and expects you to do. Besides, I was tired. I lay down, pulled up the gray blanket and in a moment was fast asleep.

I woke to a faint light in the little outside window and the sound of a key in my cell. A smiling woman, holding my clothes, walked into the room.

"Good morning, Carmen," she said. "Your parents are here to take you home."

"What happened?" I asked as I hurried into my clothes. This matron seemed like a good Joe, not an ogre like the one last night.

"Your parents came down early this morning and got you released. They're waiting downstairs for you. Good thing this is the first time you ran away, or there might be further questions." She smiled and patted me on the back. "Guess you're glad to be getting out?"

"Am I ever!"

I could hardly wait to see my folks. I fairly ran down the stairs, and there they were, standing in the hall.

"Mom," I yelled and ran up to her and threw my arms around her. I didn't wait for her to respond, I turned to Dad and hugged him too. "Oh, Dad, I'm so sorry." I waited for his arm to come around me, but it didn't.

"Carmen, what'd you run away for?" he started off, sternly. Then he looked up and saw the smiling matron. Immediately, his arm came around me and he beamed at her.

"Well, we certainly appreciate you looking after our bad little girl," he said.

The matron nodded approvingly and said, "Well, even in the best of homes, I guess the present generation misunderstands every once in a while. Hope everything works out all right."

"Oh, it will," Dad assured her. "It will. Come on, Carmen," And I felt his arm tighten around my shoulder as he more or less pushed me out of the room.

"What do these kids want anyway?" Mom muttered. "We give her three good meals a day and a warm place to sleep." Dad frowned at her, and she shut up. The smiling matron had followed us through the door and was watching our exit.

I felt a chill. Only the kind matron had gotten my father's arm around me. Already my mother was complaining. These two jerks didn't know what love was about. Wouldn't I ever have anyone who would have love, concern and understanding for me? Fleetingly, I thought maybe that last matron might have? She was kind.

We were in the parking lot when Dad took his arm off my shoulder and grabbed my wrist in a tight grip. I tried to jerk away, but he held on tight. We got into the car, and I thought bleakly, well, here I am leaving one jail, but I'm heading right into another—maybe worse?

The drive from Youth House to our house was a short one, but Dad made a detour. He stopped in the middle of the block, and said, "Wait here, I'll be right back," and disappeared into a store. When I read the sign, LIQUORS, my heart plummeted. I could taste the fear; it was worse than what I'd felt toward that awful matron. He'd kill me for sure this time! Again my thoughts went to the smiling matron. What if I'd told her about Dad's drinking? About him beating Mom up? About choking me? Would she have helped me?

In a few minutes, Dad came trotting out with the familiar brown paper sack—his God, his whiskey. We drove on home, without a word from anyone.

I hardly got in the front door before Dad locked it behind me. He didn't say a word, just walked into the kitchen and yanked a glass out of the cupboard. I watched him take the bottle out of the sack and pour a generous portion. He gulped that down and poured another. As he poured the third, I ran to my bedroom and slammed the door. In my fright, I fumbled with the lock, but it was too late—I heard him on the other side.

"Come on outta there, you dirty little tramp!" he yelled. Frantically, I tried to push some furniture against the door, but it was too late. He pushed it open, grabbed me by the arm and dragged me out into the kitchen.

Still holding me by the arm, he poured another drink from the open bottle and downed it. Then he threw out his chest and, like a soldier on parade, marched me into the living room.

"Sit down," he roared. I was like somebody in a trance. Obediently, I sat down on a chair and watched him unnotch his belt and take it off. I knew he was loaded and I was in serious trouble, but I couldn't move.

"Get up," he said, and I got up. Dad grabbed my arm with one hand and the belt whistled through the air. I felt a sting on my bottom. His aim wasn't too good. He cursed, and lifted the belt again. This time it came squarely across my back. I gritted my teeth; I wouldn't cry, no matter what —even if he killed me.

The belt kept rising and falling, and with every slash he waited for an outcry from me. When it didn't come, he cursed and flailed harder. Finally, he realized I wasn't going to give in, so he dropped the belt and threw me across a chair. I felt a sharp pain in my leg as it caught on the arm. Sprawled on the floor I watched him pick up the belt again and aim it at my face. I tried to duck, but it caught the edge of my cheek.

The pain was blinding. My fingers flew up to my cheek as the belt lifted again, and I felt the blood trickle down. Then Mom grabbed his arm.

"Enough! you've almost killed her."

But his rage was beyond control. "I'll kill her so she'll never run away again," he yelled. But Mom jumped in front of me and the belt landed on her.

That sobered him for a minute, and that minute was enough for me to scramble up and dash into the bedroom. This time, I locked the door firmly.

I stood in front of the pretty vanity and stared into the mirror, watching the blood run down my face. I hadn't cried, though. I hurt all over, but I was glad. He had beaten me, but he hadn't licked me. And he knew it.

In a few minutes, I heard footsteps into the kitchen again. I could picture him tilting the bottle, pouring the liquor into the glass. By now, maybe he was drinking right out of the bottle. He had to drink *before* he beat me, to get his nerve up, and he had to drink *after* he beat me, to calm his nerves down.

I sat down on my bed. Last night I had sat on a cot in solitary confinement. Tonight I was in my own lovely room, sitting on my own canopied bed. What was the difference?

I looked at my torn blouse. I examined the blood stains on my fingers and cheek as though they were on a stranger. I reached up and felt my cheek. It was sore—I was sore all over—inside and out.

I can't stand jails. I knew it wouldn't be long before I would run away again.

CHAPTER • 2

ABOUT SIX MONTHS later, I ran away again. Dad, as usual, had a bad day at the office, and he came in loaded, carrying his familiar brown paper sack. Also, as usual, he and Mom got into a fight. By eight o'clock, I was fed up and wondering when he'd start in on me, so I slipped out the front door and went over to Cathy Lang's house.

When Cathy answered my ring, I blurted out my problems at home and she drew me into the hall.

"Take off your coat," she said, "and come on in and meet my parents."

I was embarrassed, but there wasn't anything else I could do, so into the living room we walked. Both Cathy's Mom and Dad were understanding and kind, so I poured out all my troubles.

"I'll just give your mother a ring," Mr. Lang said finally, "so she won't worry about you. And we'll see if maybe you can spend the night here with Cathy. How would that be?"

"Oh, wonderful," I said, with relief. Anything—just so I didn't have to go back to that house. I knew Dad would beat me up if I did.

He came back after a few minutes and said Mom had consented. Then he started to tell a story—to get my mind off my troubles, I guess. Pretty soon we were all laughing and joking.

Cathy got up and wandered over to the fireplace. She stood in front of the flames for a minute or so, letting the heat warm her. As she turned to go back to her chair, her father reached out a lazy arm and pulled her down into his lap. It looked so funny. Cathy was about five-foot-six and her father wasn't much taller, yet he cuddled her like a child.

"This is my baby," he chuckled, and kissed her cheek.

I watched the two, father and daughter, with a mixture of delight and envy. If only my father felt that way about me! The only time Dad ever put his arms around me was to get a better grip, while he was beating or choking me.

That night, when Cathy and I went to bed, we talked for a long time about school, music, etcetera. Finally we got on the subject of families—kids we knew, my family, her family.

"Did you ever get a beating?" I asked Cathy.

"Of course, I've had spankings," she laughed, "when I was a kid. Who hasn't?"

"Spankings?" I was incredulous.

"Sure." Cathy nodded her head emphatically. "And believe me, Carmen, when Dad spanked me, I didn't forget it in a hurry! He made quite a production out of it.

"First, he would sit down with me and tell me what I had done wrong and why I needed a spanking. Then he'd look me right in the eye and say, 'Remember, I'm not spanking you in anger; I'm only doing it because I always want you to be a good girl. And spanking is the only way I know of that will help you to remember to do right. Don't forget when I spank you with my hand, it hurts me, too. Just as it hurts me to have you do wrong.'

"Then he'd turn me over his knee and spank me. His hands were pretty sensitive, and sometimes his hand would get pretty red. Once it even got swollen. Never as red as my bottom, though!

"When he felt I'd had enough, he'd turn me right side up, put his arms around me and tell me how much he loved me. Somehow, that always made me feel worse than the spanking. But his method sure worked. I never forgot the spanking or the wrongdoing, and it made me want to do right."

Inwardly, I marveled at her story. If she'd ever seen my dad in one of his drunken rages, she sure would have felt worse. I don't know whether she'd have wanted to do right or not.

"When's the last time you got a spanking?" I asked her.

"Oh, not for a long time—a couple of years, I guess. As I got older, I was able to communicate with both Dad and Mom much better. I love my parents and I know they love me, so it's easy to talk to each other."

She said that last with so much assurance. What a wonderful feeling to have, to love and be loved.

"Go on, tell me more about your family," I begged.

"Well. . . . We've always been a sharing family and do most things together. We go out to dinner once a week or so. Of course, that's a break for Mom, but Dad and I enjoy it too. We take turns picking out restaurants. Each of us has his own favorite, naturally, but once in a while we go hog wild and try really exotic places—Japanese or Syrian or Turkish.

"Then, there're vacations. Even when I was pretty

small, Mom and Dad included me in all the planning. Dad would come home with a whole stack of maps and brochures. After dinner, we'd spread them all out on the floor, kneel down and go over them together. It was as much fun, almost, deciding where to go and what to do, as actually going and doing.

"Sometimes, naturally, we'd get into long wrangles: Mom wanted to go to the shore, Dad to the mountains, and I on a boat trip. Eventually, we'd decide by weeding out together, and wherever we went—mountains, seashore, whatever—we always had fun."

I swallowed the lump in my throat and brushed back the few tears that trickled down my cheek.

"Boy, I sure wish I had parents like yours!"

Cathy reached over and patted my shoulder. "Don't cry, Carmen," she said. "Maybe, someday, your folks will change."

Maybe . . . someday. . . .

"Do you ever go to church?" Cathy changed the subject.

"Church? Me? No. Do you?"

"Sure, I've gone all my life. I gave my life to Christ when I was just a kid, and, believe me, it is really different when Christ lives in your heart and home."

"What do you mean? Lives in your heart and home?"

"Just that," Cathy said simply. "The Bible says '. . . Christ in you, the hope of glory.' And I have invited Christ to live in my heart."

I was flabbergasted. Of course, I'd heard about Jesus, but He seemed very far away. How could He be in your heart?

"Tell me more," I said.

"There's another Scripture verse in John 1:12 that says: 'But as many as received him [Christ], to them gave he power to become the sons of God.' I have actually experienced that, Carmen, in that I have received Christ and He lives within me."

She paused for a minute, and then added, "The wonderful thing is you can receive Christ too. It's very simple."

I was puzzled, but as Cathy went into further detail, it all sounded very possible—even plausible and *real.* I had never heard of this *receiving* before, but I felt a great desire to know Jesus—to really receive Him in my heart.

"Let's pray together," Cathy suggested.

She prayed just a simple prayer. But, as she prayed, tears started to run down her cheeks and she placed her hand in mine. Never, in my life, had I felt such concern and compassion from another person. As long as I live, I shall never forget her prayer. It went something like this:

> Lord Jesus, please help Carmen right now. Help her to know that You love her and that You died for her so that she might enjoy life. I pray for her parents now, too, dear Lord. Help them to understand there can be complete happiness in Christ. Jesus, You said that You have come to give us life and that more abundantly. Help Carmen to come to know You as her personal Saviour and King of her life. I pray also, Dear Jesus, that as Carmen goes home tomorrow You will help her to be God's best. Help her to live for You. In Your name I pray, in the name of Jesus. Amen.

By the time she finished, I was crying, too. I asked her to tell me about her church and she told me that her parents had been saved at a Billy Graham Crusade in New York City. Afterwards, a local pastor, the Reverend Brown, had visited them and invited them to his church.

Cathy liked the pastor there and was secretary of a very active youth group. Her mother and father were youth advisors. I wished I could feel as proud as Cathy of my parents, my pastor, my church—proud of anything or anyone.

"Why don't you come to church with me next Sunday?" Cathy asked.

I agreed and with that we went to sleep.

Next morning, Saturday, the smell of bacon frying wakened me. Both of us lay there for a few minutes, savoring the smell and putting off getting up. Finally, our appetites got the best of us and we dressed and went into the kitchen, where her parents were starting in on bacon, eggs, toast, jelly and coffee.

Oh, how I longed to stay! But I knew I'd have to leave around noon, even before Cathy suggested it.

It was about one o'clock when I walked into our place. Neither Mom nor Dad had much to say. I was dying for them to say something—anything—so I could tell them a thing or two—about Cathy's life: how her parents really cared; how they went to church together; the easy way they all had with each other; how they could talk together. Yes, I was prepared, but I didn't get the chance. Probably a good thing, too, as I'm sure Dad would have used *his* method of communication and wound up beating me.

Next day I went to church with the Langs, and my parents let me spend the day with them. That evening we went back to church, and I had the same feeling, sitting in that church, that I'd had when Cathy prayed for me. How I wished that my parents were sitting there with me!

After church, we stopped for hamburgers and milk shakes. Oh, how I hated to go home! It was so good, so natural, being with the Langs; they made me really want to live. At home, I didn't care much whether I lived or died.

I attended church with them for a few more Sundays, and each time I reminded my parents how much I'd like them to go. I guess my harping on how nice Cathy's parents were is what finally teed Dad off. Anyway, he told Mom he didn't want me going to the Langs' anymore.

"She's turning into a religious nut!" he said. "All I hear from morning to night is the Langs this and the Langs that. Or how wonderful Pastor Brown is. She'll turn into a crackpot for sure. I don't want her going there."

I begged both Mom and Dad to go to church with me, so they could see that the place wasn't full of nuts, that they were all wonderful people. But Dad flatly refused.

"Sunday's the only day I have time to do a lot of things that need doing around the house," he replied.

What a laugh! He slept late every Sunday, drank the afternoon away, and watched television after dinner.

From that time on, my interest in everything faded. I didn't care about clothes, or records, or school. My grades began to slip and I caught the devil for that, too. Life seemed hardly worth living; it was just a matter of existing.

CHAPTER • 3

THEN LULU, an eighteen-year-old girl who lived just up the street, got real friendly. Although I was younger than she, we seemed to have a lot in common—trouble with parents, problems at school. We started to see a lot of each other.

One Saturday evening Lulu called and asked if I'd like to go for a ride. Mom said it was all right, so I said, "Sure."

She picked me up a little after 7:30, and after I got into the car, she asked, "How'd you like to go to Manhattan?"

"Why not?"

On the way there, Lulu told me she had friends in upper Manhattan. "I've been driving in to see them most Saturday nights. We have some good times together. I think you'll like them," she said.

When we reached Broadway and 116th Street, she turned into a dark side street and parked the car. It wasn't the best part of town, and I got a little scared.

The streets were filthy, and the garbage cans in front of the run-down tenements spilled over onto both sidewalk and street. Lulu led me into the lobby of one of the houses, and I looked around curiously. It was obvious that, at one time, this building had been a fairly nice apartment house.

But now the marble floors hadn't been cleaned for months, and the cracking, stippled walls hadn't seen paint for longer than that.

A boarded-over hole yawned where the elevator had been, and we walked over to the dilapidated stairs and began to climb up and up—past the second floor, past the third.

"Where are you taking me?" I panted as we toiled on past the fourth floor.

"To a friend of mine, as I told you. Don't worry, nothing's going to happen to you," Lulu snapped and she started to climb faster and faster. She was almost skipping every other step.

By the time we got to the fifth floor, I was too out of breath to protest anymore.

"C'mon, you're in for a great surprise," Lulu announced and led me down the hall to Apartment 5-C.

I heard laughing inside, and then, as Lulu rang, footsteps. The boy who opened the door had long blond hair and a short beard; he looked around twenty.

"Lulu, Baby, come in!" He boomed. He threw his arms around her and hugged and kissed her.

"And who's this you've got here?"

"Oh, this is Carmen, Marty," Lulu said.

"Hey, you're really a swingin' thing!" he grinned, as his eyes took me in from head to foot. Then he laughed that big booming laugh again and enveloped me in a bear hug.

His arm dropped to my waist, as we walked down the long, narrow hall. The reassuring grip was comforting. What was coming next?

"Something new has been added," Marty announced to the group in the dimly lit living room. "You all know Lulu, but. . . ." he paused dramatically. "For the very first time, it is my profound, distinct and honorable pleasure to introduce to you one of the greatest—Carmen."

The applause was loud, and I offered a tentative smile, as I tried to make out the occupants of the room. I couldn't see very well; the only light was from a candle and from a red and green lamp. There was a strong, smoky smell in the air. It was like nothing I'd smelled before—not like cigarette smoke, exactly, but sweeter than that.

I made out a number of what looked like teen-agers, lying here and there on the floor. Some were half-dressed.

An attractive blonde girl, sitting in a corner, motioned me to come over.

"Hi, Carmen. I'm Bonnie," she said, as I sat down beside her. "You'll have a great time. It's always nice to have one more."

Now that my eyes were accustomed to the dimness, I could see that everyone *did* look happy. Some of the girls were laughing at the offhand remarks the boys were making. Next to me, a boy and girl were so locked in an embrace, they were oblivious to everyone there. I was more than a little shocked at their behavior before such an audience, and Bonnie noticed my expression.

"Don't let them bother you," she said. "They just had a stick together, and I guess it turned them on. It does for some. Man, when you get to feeling that way, you want to do a lot of things you've never thought of before. I guess that's their thing."

As she saw that her words did little to relieve my discomfort, she pointed tactfully to the other side of the room.

"See that girl over there, feeling up and down the wall? She is high on acid. She's *really* out of it."

Through the smoke I made out the girl. She acted as though she were picking flowers off the wallpaper. First, she plucked one, then she smelled it and finally she stuck it in her hair. As she turned her back to the wall and began to rub herself up and down against the flowers, a boy walked by and she reached out for him.

Oh, oh, I thought to myself, here they go. But all she did was grab his arm. He smiled at her and she let go and returned to her flower picking.

"What happened then?" I asked Bonnie.

"You *never* want to get *that* way when you're on acid," she replied. "You can really go out of your mind, if you do. I'll never forget a trip I had, when I tried some monkey business."

"What?" I was completely fascinated.

"Well, I had just dropped some acid and I got this feeling, so I latched onto a guy. Believe me, I had all kinds of feelings. I was high above the earth, heading for the moon. Then I stopped and sat on some clouds. Finally I fell, right into the center of the earth, into a lake of fire. I can't describe the pain. I screamed at the boy and told him I was on fire and begged him to put it out. He grabbed my fingers and pulled hard on one at a time. Each time it felt as though a finger were coming off, and each time one was pulled off, I screamed. It seemed an eternity, but finally the fire went out. Believe me, I've never gone near a boy, when I'm playing with acid, since. I can still feel that fire and pain."

A boy sitting next to Bonnie leaned over and offered her a cigarette. I remembered the film we'd had in school on narcotics. I was sure this cigarette was marijuana; it didn't look like an ordinary one.

Bonnie nodded her thanks, lit the cigarette, took a deep breath, held it, then slowly exhaled.

"Want to try it?" she asked.

I looked at the cigarette she held out to me with fascination and fear. I remembered the school movies, but I also remembered the stories kids who had smoked marijuana had told me. It makes you feel good all over; it gets all the hell, hate and rebellion out of you.

What did I have to lose? I reached over and took the cigarette from Bonnie's hand.

I put it in my mouth, inhaled and exhaled. Nothing happened. I looked at Bonnie questioningly.

"No, no," she laughed. "Not so fast. When you inhale, hold it so the smoke drops to your lungs. Hold it as long as you can, then exhale slowly. Give the smoke a chance to penetrate your whole body."

I took another long puff, inhaled and held it. As I exhaled, I felt a light, tingling sensation. I took another puff, and another. Each time felt better than the last.

How does it feel? It's like coming home after being away on a long trip; like eating when you've had no food in a long time; like finding money when you're broke; like buying a new dress; like Christmas. All the good things—everything is good and nothing matters a great deal.

By the time I finished my first stick, I never wanted the sensation to stop. Finally, I had found the answer—marijuana.

In the meantime, Lulu had long since gotten high. The last I had seen of her, she and Marty had been heading for the bedroom, arms entwined about each other.

By the time Lulu reappeared, alone, I was coming down

off my high and getting a little scared. I didn't want to mess around with a boy, and the more I thought about it, the more frightened I got.

I looked at my watch. It was after midnight; my folks would have a fit! I got up and walked over to Lulu.

"Let's go," I said. "It's late, and I'll catch the devil when I get home."

On our way home, all I could think of was what my folks would say. I knew it would take about forty-five minutes to get there, and all I could do was hope desperately that they'd both be in bed.

But I wasn't that lucky. When Lulu pulled up in front of our house, every light in the house was on. I knew trouble was ahead, but I took a deep breath, hopped out of the car, ran up the steps, and opened the front door, slowly.

Mom and Dad were sitting in the living room watching television. There were empty beer bottles standing on the coffee table.

"Where have *you* been?" Dad roared, the minute he saw me.

I couldn't tell them the truth, that was for sure. I groped for an answer, but Dad didn't give me a chance.

"Out with that girl Lulu!" he said, and shook his finger at me. "You know you've no business running around with her. She comes from a bad home and has a bad reputation with the boys. Nothing but a little tramp. You've been with a boy, Carmen, haven't you?" he accused.

That really shocked me; at least I wouldn't be lying about that. "Why, Dad, that's not true at all. We were over at Betsy's house, watching TV," I lied.

"You dirty, rotten little liar! We called Betsy's house over an hour ago. Here it is a quarter of two. Girl, you *have* been up to something bad. And lying besides."

He reached out and grabbed the top of my blouse. As I tried to duck, I heard the material give and felt the blouse rip open.

Dad was cursing all the while. "I'll teach you to play around with men," he yelled. "I'll beat you naked so you'll never go near another boy."

And with that he let go of the scrap of blouse in his hand and lunged for my skirt. The material didn't give, so he gave a violent jerk, and I went sprawling to the floor. Before I could recover, he leaped on me and tore at the skirt, but it was made of pretty sturdy stuff and it didn't rip.

I was so stunned, I couldn't even fight back, but then Mom piled in and tried to pull Dad off me.

"That's no way to solve her sex problems," she pleaded. "Beating her to death isn't going to help her any."

Mom's sudden attack gave me a chance to get my breath back and to realize that I was fighting for my life. I raked Dad across the face with my nails, but he just slapped me back. Frantically, I tried to crawl, but he clung to my back like a leech. Finally, I rolled over and over. That shook him off and I took off for the kitchen like a frightened deer.

"Come back here, you little devil," Dad screamed as he lunged to his feet, but I kept running. I was sure if I could make it out the back door, he wouldn't chase me down the street.

It took a trillion years to reach that door, but I finally got it open. I heard a lamp crash behind me—Dad must have thrown it at me. As the door slammed shut behind me, I heard him bellow: "Carmen, if I ever get my hands on you, I'll choke every last breath out of your lying little body!"

I kept running and running, around the side of the house

and down the street. I knew Dad couldn't catch me, but it seemed to my frightened mind that the faster I ran, the farther away I would get from all my troubles.

Out of breath at last, I collapsed under a tree on someone's lawn. My lungs ached for air, my trembling legs would carry me no farther. How long I lay there, I don't know, but finally some strength returned and I knew I had to think about where to go.

Home was out of the question. Never would I set foot in that place again! I thought of Cathy's house. No, that wouldn't do. Cathy and her parents had been wonderful to me, but how could I show up there, all disheveled, at this hour of the morning?

Lulu? Yes, maybe Lulu would take me in; she would look after me.

I got up and looked around. Actually, I wasn't half as far away from home as I'd thought. The Berquist's yard, where I'd collapsed, was only about ten blocks from our house. Lulu's place was beyond ours, but I didn't want to take a chance, so I walked over a couple of blocks, turned right and headed for Lulu's.

When I got there, I couldn't decide what to do. I didn't want to waken her parents, so I crept up to her window and knocked gently.

"Lulu," I called. "Lulu, please wake up. It's me—Carmen. I need you."

I waited for what seemed hours. No response. I knocked again, and finally Lulu pulled up her shade.

"Carmen, for heaven's sake. . . ."

"Let me in, Lulu," I pleaded. "My old man kicked me out. I've nowhere else to go. Can you let me stay here tonight?"

She looked nonplussed, but finally said, "Well, sure. Go around to the front door and I'll let you in. But be quiet."

By the time I reached the front door, Lulu had it open and was standing there, yawning.

"Come in, come in," she whispered impatiently. Then, "What in the world ever happened to you?"

I looked down. Half of my blouse was gone; my skirt was half-down, half-up from the tussle—only the button held it up—the zipper was hanging loose.

"Oh," I breathed with relief, as she led me back to her room. "My old man tried to beat me up for—oh, sex, a whole lot of other things. You name it. He finally. . . ."

"Sssh," Lulu whispered, and put her finger to her lips. "Don't wake Mom up; she's not in very good shape. I'll tell you later."

When Lulu opened the door to her room, I felt truly at home. It was fully as messy as mine. Magazines were strewn on the floor; clothes on the dresser, odd shoes here and there on the floor. . . .

"Tell me what happened," she said, "but keep it down. Mom is really in pretty bad shape; my old man met another woman in a bar about a month ago and he hasn't been home since. She's taking it kind of hard."

She reached into her bureau drawer, pulled out a pair of pajamas and tossed them to me. I reached up to take off my tattered blouse, and my father's rage-filled face came before me.

"You fiend, I hope to God you kill yourself," I yelled, as I threw the blouse at the wall with all my might.

"Sshh," Lulu warned again. "Be quiet or Mom'll hear and then we'll be in trouble."

"I'm sorry, Lulu. I sure do appreciate you taking me in,

but every time I think of my father, rage explodes inside me. I hate him with every inch of my guts. Maybe I express it the wrong way, but that's the God's honest truth," I said, as I finished undressing and put on the pajamas.

We got into Lulu's double bed and started to talk, but I was exhausted. My mind kept going but my tongue gave out. Fortunately for me, Lulu fell asleep soon, and I lay there trying to quiet my thoughts so sleep could come.

I slept soundly, and it was quite late when we got up. By the time I walked into the kitchen Lulu had told her mother about me and her mother had said I could stay. She left shortly after I got up to begin her daily search for a job. Lulu said, since her father had left, money was really scarce. The welfare department helped some, but not enough.

Lulu and I had some breakfast, just toast and coffee; I didn't feel like eating much. Then I called my mother. I barely had time to get out "Hi, Mom," before she started in.

"I suppose by now you're sorry for what you've done," she said.

"Sorry?" I was boiling mad. "Sorry for what? Sorry that Dad ripped my blouse? Sorry he kicked me out? I'm glad. As far as I'm concerned I don't care if I never see him again! And the sooner you get rid of that drunken bum, the better off you'll be."

"Carmen, don't you dare talk about your father that way," Mom yelled at me. "You're responsible for what he's done and all that's happened to him. He's in the hospital right now because of you."

"What?" I couldn't believe my ears. "Because of me! What did I do? He was trying to kill me, and all I did was get away. Did the disappointment give him a heart attack?"

"When you ran out of the house, he fell over the lamp table and broke his leg. God knows how long he'll be there. If he loses his job, you're responsible!"

"Listen, you old bag," I screamed into the phone. "I've had it. I'm not taking any more lip from either one of you any more." And I banged up the receiver.

Lulu walked in, just as I hung up. "Well," she drawled, "sounds like a war going on. Mom and I have fights, too, once in a while. She's scared of me, though, so she usually backs down."

We lazed around most of the day, listening to the radio and talking. Late that afternoon, Lulu's mother came in and said she'd landed a job as a waitress and would be on the four-to-midnight shift that night.

"Well, I'm glad you finally got something," Lulu said. "But I'll need the car tonight."

"I need the car to get to work," her mother protested, but Lulu didn't give an inch.

She just kept repeating, "Sorry, I really have to have the car."

Finally, her mother gave in and said she'd take the bus. After her mother left, I asked Lulu why she needed the car.

"Well, you can see Mom and I don't have much," she explained. "And it'll be a few days at least before Mom gets paid. I have a friend who said he'd help me out any time I needed it, and I figure we all three need it now—right? So I'm going to run over to see him. I'd take you with me, but it might be a little embarrassing for all of us. I'll be right back—only take a few minutes. OK?"

I was touched. "Why, sure," I said. "I'll just stay here and watch TV."

"Back in twenty minutes," Lulu called, as she went out the front door.

Two hours later, she was still gone. When she finally did come back, she was very apologetic.

"I'm so sorry I'm late. This guy wasn't home, and I didn't know what to do, so I just sat in the car and waited. When he finally did get there, he let me have twenty-five dollars until Mom gets paid. You do understand, don't you?"

"Of course," I said, but she kept right on until I began to get suspicious. Why did she explain so much? But then she sat down before the TV with me, and I dismissed it all from my mind.

It wasn't long before her head started to nod.

"Lulu, why don't you go to bed?" I asked.

"I'm really not sleepy, just a little tired," she insisted, but her eyelids were half-closed as she leaned over and asked, "Carmen, you happy?"

"Happy? Of course I'm not happy. What difference does that make?"

"I'm happy!" She almost caroled the words.

"Because of the money you got to help out your mother?"

Lulu laughed. "You want to be happy, Carmen?"

"What are you getting at?" I couldn't make head nor tail of her attitude, then it dawned on me: "Oh, now, I get it! You must have some marijuana. Boy, I could sure use a stick right now." I looked at her hopefully.

"I can get you *real* happy," she replied. She reached into her bra and pulled out a little cellophane bag.

I stared at it, as she dangled it before me. What is it?"

"Smack."

"Smack—what's smack?"

"You gotta be kiddin'," Lulu snorted. "You've gotta know what smack is—stuff, heroin. Sometimes they use other names for it. Whatever they call it, it sure cures your troubles."

Heroin? But only real drug addicts took that! "Lulu," I said, "you never told me you were an addict. My God, I've heard what happens to people who take heroin."

"Drug addict? I'm no drug addict," she laughed. "I only take the stuff to get my mind off my troubles. I can take it or leave it. Not me, I'm no addict. I can handle it."

I couldn't help being inquisitive. Last night I'd had marijuana, and it had made me feel great. Tonight, my troubles were worse. What would smack do for me? Marijuana hadn't hurt, so why not give it a try? I needed some kind of escape. Maybe heroin would provide it.

"OK, give me some."

"I've only got one bag left," Lulu said, "but I know where I can get more. C'mon, let's go see my friend."

We got into the car and headed for Brooklyn. Lulu started humming; she didn't seem very talkative any more. Finally I asked her, "Is this the same fellow who gave you the twenty-five dollars?"

"*Gave* me twenty-five bucks? Sorry, kiddo, I told you a big, fat lie. I made forty dollars and spent fifteen dollars for stuff."

"How'd you make forty dollars so quickly," I asked.

Lulu laughed. "You really are a big sap, aren't you? You've got something men'll pay a lot of money for. I've got a couple of friends who told me anytime I need money to go to them. So I saw two last night and each one gave me a twenty for my services."

It took me a few minutes to digest what she'd told me. Then I realized Lulu was a prostitute! As I thought about it, I realized I couldn't blame Lulu for the spot she was in, but I abhorred the idea of ever becoming one myself. Once, when I was only around twelve, a neighbor boy got fresh with me. I was curious and let him get away with it, but it was a degrading and embarrassing experience. I never forgot it. Other guys tried later, but I never let them.

When we got to Brooklyn, Lulu pulled up in front of a fashionable apartment house.

"This is it," she announced, as she rang one of the apartment bells.

"Who is it?" a man's voice answered.

"Hi, Bud. It's Lulu Masefield."

The buzzer rang and I followed Lulu up the steps to the second floor. She knocked on one of the doors and a small, well-built man of about thirty opened it.

"Hi, there," he said. "Who's this with you?"

"Carmen. She's living with me," she explained briefly. Then, as we walked into the apartment, she got to the point, quickly.

Bud took the ten dollars she offered, went into another room and came back with two bags of heroin, which he handed to Lulu.

"Is it okay if we use your set of works? Both of us would like to get off together." Lulu said.

"Sure, why not?"

Bud led us into the bathroom, reached in back of the toilet bowl and pulled out a small, crumpled bundle of paper. When he unwrapped the contents, I recognized the familiar tools from that movie about narcotics we were shown at school. Yes, there was the little bottle cap, the needle and eyedropper.

"Here, I'll help you. Give me both bags," Bud said, and we handed him the heroin.

Then he took off his belt and handed it to Lulu. Fascinated, I watched Bud open the two bags and dump the white powder into the bottle cap. He ran some water into a glass, then sucked the water up into the eyedropper. He squeezed the dropper of water into the powder in the bottle cap, swished up the water and powder, lit a match and heated the solution.

In the meantime, Lulu had wrapped the belt around the upper part of her arm. She started to rub the crook of her elbow. By that time Bud was ready. He inserted the end of the needle into the main vein of her arm. I watched him squeeze the end of the eyedropper. He let up on the needle and blood flowed back into the eyedropper. Then he squeezed again and half of the solution went into Lulu's arm.

I lifted my eyes from what seemed a delicate operation to Lulu's face. Drops of sweat stood on her forehead, but otherwise she looked completely relaxed.

"Man, does that feel good!" she sighed.

When Bud pulled the needle out, Lulu handed me the belt, and I tried to imitate what she had done. I was rather clumsy, and Lulu helped me tighten the belt around my arm.

"Squeeze your hand hard, and pump your veins," she advised.

I tried, and watched my own veins grow bigger and bigger; it was like looking at someone else's arm. Bud reached over, grabbed my arm and stuck the needle in. It hurt like crazy! I felt dizzy, but I gritted my teeth and closed my eyes. A few minutes later he pulled the needle out.

I waited. . . . Nothing happened—nothing that I had expected. My stomach started to turn over. I ran to the toilet bowl and retched and retched. It seemed I'd never stop vomiting.

After about fifteen minutes of retching and feeling dizzy, the heroin started to hit me. Before long, I was on cloud nine. All of my hang-ups were gone; I didn't care about Mom, Dad, my home, anything. I just wanted to have this feeling last forever; it was even better than marijuana.

The three of us returned to the living room and sat down. Bud's apartment was a far cry from Marty's. It was well furnished and neat as a pin. By now, I was completely relaxed, so I poured out all my woes to Bud.

"I sure know what you're talking about," he said. "My old man and old lady got a divorce when I was fourteen. I ran away from home a couple of times, and wound up in a juvenile home. What really threw me was the day I found out my mother was on drugs."

"You mean she was an addict?" It didn't seem possible —somebody's *mother?* "I thought the younger generation was the only one that went in for drugs."

Bud laughed. "You haven't been around much, Baby, have you? Drugs have been around for a long, long time. My mother did try to get help. Once she went to a religious place for drug addicts, and I stayed with my grandmother. It didn't last long, though. I went up to visit her one day and the staff discovered she was taking pills, so they sent us both packing—pronto. Boy, I'll never forget that! We wound up in New York City with no money and no place to stay."

"Well, what'd you do?"

"I told you my mother was quite a gal, didn't I?" Bud's grin was wry, his voice cynical. "We walked along the street for a while and then she started asking passersby for money. A few gave us some—not enough for a bed, though—and then came the real shocker, what finished me with her for good.

"One of the men who handed over a quarter, gave Ma a second look and then asked how much she charged. 'Fifteen bucks,' she replied promptly, then turned to me and said, 'Wait right here, I'll be back in a few minutes.'"

Bud's head bowed; he seemed to be struggling to continue. "That was it; we were finished, kaput. I didn't wait for her to come back. From there on out I had no father, no mother—just me."

I wanted to comfort him, but it was such a sordid story, there seemed little I could say. I reached my hand out to him and said, "I'm sorry, Bud, things turned out so bad for you. I'm kinda in the same boat now. I'm all alone too."

Bud took my hand and squeezed it gently. "Oh, I'm getting used to this alone business," he said. "It's tough at first, but don't worry, you'll make it."

"Well, I've got my old friend Lulu here, the only one who'd take me in when I was uptight. I sure appreciate it, Lulu."

Lulu smiled at me and then started to tell us the story of *her* parents, the fights she'd had with them and the hell she went through. Bud and I both nodded our heads in sympathy. I had a feeling of peace—here we were sitting like a family, two sisters and a brother, telling each other our problems.

Finally, Lulu came to an end, looked at her watch and said we'd better get going. She wanted to beat her mother home.

I told Bud how much I appreciated talking to him and he put his arm around me, drew me up close and said, "Carmen, I'm sure you and I are going to meet again."

My heart leaped and reached out to him. I wished he would never let me go. His life was like mine; we had so much in common. Was it really in the cards that we'd meet again? I certainly hoped so.

On the way home, I turned to Lulu and asked, "Does Bud have a girl friend? He really is a terrific guy."

"Bud has lots of girl friends, lots of boy friends. He's a pusher and his stuff is dynamite. Yes sirreee, everybody loves Bud! You will, too, some day. You'll love him more than anyone else in this whole wide world. Believe me, Baby, you'll get hooked on Bud, and I really mean hooked!"

CHAPTER • 4

LULU'S MOTHER was sitting on the sofa crying, when we walked in.

"Mom! What's the matter? Is the job too hard?"

"I just couldn't take it. I got the orders all mixed up; I spilled things and to top it all off, one guy propositioned me," she sobbed. "I just walked out. The boss wouldn't even pay me for the time I put in, either, said I'd have to work the whole week."

Lulu grinned when her mother mentioned being propositioned, but then she tried to reassure her.

"Aw, don't worry, Mom. Something'll turn up and it'll all work out OK."

"But we haven't a cent!" her mother wailed. "There's rent to pay and other bills. No food in the house. What are we to do?"

I squirmed as she looked up at me. I wasn't helping her money problems any. I was adding to them by being an extra mouth to feed. It made me feel awful.

Lulu walked over and patted her mother. "Don't worry, Mom, everything's going to be all right. I've got a little change. I'll go to the store in the morning and pick up a few things."

I followed Lulu into her bedroom and said, "Maybe I should leave. I'm just another problem if I stay on."

"Oh, cut it out, Carmen. You're no problem. Mom'll get over it, and I can always take care of her. This new job I got pays real well." Lulu smirked as she drew a twenty dollar bill out of her bra.

It seemed incredible that anyone could make money so easily. Maybe I could do the same? The thought sent a chill down my spine. How could I sell my body? Oh, God, please don't let that happen to me, I prayed silently.

I climbed into bed beside Lulu and, thankfully, this night sleep came quickly.

Next morning we had milk and corn flakes for breakfast. That's all there was in the house. After cleaning up, we walked to a nearby grocery and loaded up with twenty dollars worth of food.

As we neared her house, I asked Lulu, "How are you going to explain this much money to your mother?"

"Oh, I'll think of something. Don't worry. Just keep your mouth shut about what really happened."

We marched into the kitchen and plunked the full bags down on the kitchen table in front of Lulu's mother, who was having a cup of coffee.

"Where in the world did you get these groceries?" she asked.

"In the grocery store. Where do you suppose?"

"I mean where did you get the money?"

"Don't worry, I didn't steal it. Actually you'll never believe it, but this is what happened. Just as we reached the corner I noticed my shoelace was untied. I stooped to tie it and there in the gutter was a twenty-dollar bill! At first

I thought it was play money; it was all crumpled and dirty but when I picked it up, it was for true! I even showed i to Carmen, and she said it was real, too. Boy, were w excited!"

"Well, honey," her mother smiled, "I guess this goo luck happened to us because we been livin' right." An with no further questions, her mother started to put th food away.

As the day wore on, Lulu complained of a headache. Sh was very irritable and snapped at both of us. At lunch sh cussed her mother out because the hamburgers were to rare. At dinner she cussed me for not passing the beans fas enough.

Right after dinner, Lulu announced that she and I wer going to a show. I watched Lulu change into a real mini mini skirt and a white, low-necked sweater.

"What show are we going to?" I asked as we pulled awa from the curb.

"You really are a babe," Lulu said. "Did you really thin we were going to a show? I've gotta' get straight. Yo might as well know it, Carmen, I'm hooked. And if I don' get something right away I'm going to be sicker than a dog I got up long before you this morning and got off. Now need it again, but bad!"

Was it just last night that Lulu had said, "I'm no dru addict—I can take it or leave it—I can handle it"? I looke at her carefully. She didn't look any different—not upse or nervous or anything. It was hard to believe she reall was an addict. I didn't know what to say or do.

Lulu parked on Fourth and Atlantic and got out of th car. "Wait here, I'll be right back," she said.

I watched her walk to the corner, cross to the other sid

of the street, and stop and lean against the wall of a small cafeteria. She just stood there for a while, watching people walk by. I was just beginning to lose interest when a man stopped and spoke to her. Then they walked off together and disappeared around the corner.

My heart pounded like a trip-hammer. Even though I had seen it with my own eyes, I couldn't believe a girl could really do something like that! I kept my eyes glued to the corner, and in about half an hour she appeared around the corner. I heaved a sigh of relief. Now, we could get going again.

But she took up her post by the cafeteria again and soon another man spoke to her. They talked for a few minutes and then the guy walked on alone. A few minutes later another man stopped, and this time Lulu went with him.

I was beginning to get scared. How long would I have to sit here? But I was also fascinated at how easily Lulu picked up these men; it seemed just too simple.

"Hey there!" a voice came through the open window. A man was standing there, leering at me. Oh, my God, I thought, he thinks I'm a prostitute.

"Get away from me," I screamed.

"Aw, lady, all I want is a dime for a cuppa coffee," he whined, and I realized he was just a harmless drunk.

"Get out before I call the cops," I snapped, and wound up the window and snapped the door locks.

The man shrugged and lurched away. Just then Lulu appeared, and this time, thank goodness, she headed for the car. I reached over and unsnapped the lock on the driver's side: she jumped in and we drove off.

"Gee," she said, "I was afraid one of those guys was a cop, but he just walked on and didn't make anything of it, so I guess he wasn't. It wasn't a bad evening," she added. "Ten from the first guy and fifteen from the second. Let's go see Bud, huh?"

Bud? I wasn't going to argue with her about that. My pulse quickened at the mere thought of him. What was it I liked about him? His personality? His looks? His clothes? Our mutual problems? I didn't know. I didn't care. I think I was in love with him.

We parked in the same spot as the night before and walked hurriedly into his apartment house and rang the buzzer. Both of us were anxious to see him again—for entirely different reasons.

When Bud answered Lulu's ring at the door, he looked just as wonderful as I had imagined.

"Come on in, come on in," he said, with a great big smile. "Glad to see you again, Carmen. Hi, Lulu."

He remembered my name! And he greeted me first!

Again Lulu wasted no time: "I want five bags," she said.

Bud walked into the bedroom and handed her the bags, as she held out the money. Then she walked into the bathroom and Bud and I sat down on the sofa. I was dying to talk to someone about Lulu's behavior tonight, so I spilled it all out to him. He didn't say anything for a few moments, and then, much to my surprise, he ignored my remarks altogether.

"Did you go back home today?" he asked.

"No. I'm never going back there."

"Never?"

"Never," I said firmly. "I'd rather die first."

"Listen," he said. He leaned over confidentially. "If you ever get in a tight spot and need a place to stay, you can come here. I've thought about what you told me last night, and I really think you've had a pretty rough time. If I can help any time, I'll be glad to."

"You mean stay right here? With you?"

Bud nodded.

"But. . . . but . . . ?"

He laughed. "Don't worry. That sofa you're sitting on folds out into a real comfortable bed. I'll sleep in the bedroom and you can bunk up here."

"You really mean that?" My mind could hardly picture how wonderful it would be to stay in a snazzy place like this, and with Bud, too. What more could a girl ask for?

"Sure," he grinned. "You can be my kid sister."

"Oh, Bud, I'll never be able to tell you how much I appreciate this!" Already I was trying to figure out how I could manage to move in here.

Then Bud put his arms around me and drew me close. He kissed me very gently.

Just then Lulu called from the bathroom. "Carmen, c'mere a minute."

I walked over and she pulled me inside and shut the door. "Want to get off?"

I looked at her and then at the needle. I knew I really shouldn't, but she smiled at me and I remembered that wonderful feeling of last night.

I nodded and she prepared the fix for me, and knotted a nylon around my arm. As I puffed up my veins and watched her stick the needle in, I wondered if I was going to throw up again. This time, the solution went right in, and as Lulu pulled the needle out I reached over and kissed her on the cheek. The reaction was already coming—the peace, the euphoria.

"Man, that sure feels good," I sighed. "This is really a

great night for me. I think Bud's in love with me."

I visualized myself as Bud's girl—cooking for him, cleaning for him, just being *his* girl.

Lulu said nothing, just busied herself washing off the needle and putting the works back into her purse. Then she opened the door and we returned to the living room.

"Look, Lulu," Bud said, and he sounded angry. "Next time you want to get off here, ask me. OK?"

"C'mon, let's go," Lulu said to me, and headed for the door without saying anything to Bud.

Bud walked to the door with us, but this time the good-byes were brief. I wanted to say something to try to smooth things over, but no words seemed to fit.

"That stinking pig!" Lulu said furiously, as we got into her car. "He just wants my money and that's it. He had no business getting mad over me getting off there."

I sprang to Bud's defense. "Well, Lulu, I suppose you should have asked."

"Nuts to that! If I knew another place to get good stuff, I'd never go back to that lousy apartment."

"Lulu, you shouldn't feel that way," I said, weakly. "You had no right to do what you did."

"Aw, mind your own business," she snapped, and I stayed quiet. But in my mind I had figured out that Bud was right. That was all that mattered. Bud was right.

By the time we got home, Lulu had quieted down. She was still mad at Bud, but the first edge of anger had worn off. She went to bed soon after we got back to the house. But I could still feel the effects of the heroin and I stayed up to keep that wonderful feeling. When I finally went into her room, she was sound asleep. I had done some thinking while I sat in the living room. I crept over and took a dollar out of Lulu's purse. I put it in my own, undressed and crawled into bed. I felt a little guilty, but I figured Lulu wouldn't miss it and I needed it for my plans. Lulu slept on.

When we got up next morning, Lulu was still mad. Her mother wasn't in too good a mood, either, with no prospects of a job or money. I figured this was the time for me to bow out.

"I guess I've changed my mind about my parents," I told Lulu. "I better go back home. Dad has probably cooled down by now, and I know Mom'll take me back."

"I know what you mean," Lulu replied. "My old lady usually gets over her bad moods too." It was obvious from her tone that she wouldn't be sorry for me to leave. Everything was working out beautifully.

"C'mon, let's have some breakfast before you go," she said. Again we had corn flakes, since the groceries we'd bought had been mostly staples and dinner stuff. Then Lulu gave me a pair of pajamas and a change of clothes.

I thanked her and her mother and started in the direction of my home. After I got a few blocks away, I turned and headed for the station and Bud!

All the long way to Brooklyn, I kept wondering what Bud would say. I rehearsed what *I* was going to say. Would he accept me? Had he really meant what he said?

I rang the buzzer, hesitantly. No answer. I rang again. Again no answer. I waited a few minutes and rang a third time.

"Hello, who is it?" It was Bud's voice! My heart raced.

"Me, Carmen."

"Carmen! What are you doing here?"

"Let me in, and I'll tell you," I said.

"Well, come on up," he said, and I heard his laugh again.

All the way up the stairs I upbraided myself. I was a liar and a thief. Last night I had stolen money from Lulu; I had lied to her and her mother. What kind of heel was I, anyway? But the thought of Bud pushed everything else out of my mind, and I had to say and do what I did or Bud might not take me in.

Bud was standing at the open door in his pajamas. "Excuse my appearance," he said, "I hadn't gotten up yet."

He led me into the living room and I spilled out all that had happened. He listened sympathetically, not saying a word. When I finally ran out of breath, he rose and asked, "How about some breakfast. If Lulu threw you out, I don't imagine you've had any?"

"No," I lied, "but, let me fix something for you."

"Eggs and ham in the refrigerator. Fry mine soft. Coffee in the cupboard on the right," Bud said. "I'll get some clothes on while you dish something up."

After we ate and I cleaned up, we returned to the living room. We spent most of the day just sitting around talking. Toward evening, the doorbell rang from time to time. Each person came for drugs. Bud had a good trade.

About nine o'clock Bud said he had to go out for a while. (I found out later that most nights he went out around this time to pick up more drugs from his connection. Then he, in turn, sold it to addicts.)

I was yawning when he returned, so he suggested I turn in.

"You've had a long day," he said. "You must be tired. I'll get some blankets from the closet and help you make up the sofa."

We made the bed up together and I went to the bathroom to change into pajamas and get ready for the night. When I came out, Bud was sitting on the chair watching TV. Since I had no robe, I was a little embarassed, so I slipped into bed quickly and pulled the covers up. Bud looked over at me and smiled, then turned back to the TV.

When the end of the program came, he turned the set off and asked if I wanted the light left on or off.

"Off, please," I said meekly.

He turned it off, gave me a brief salute and went into his bedroom and closed the door.

All sorts of thoughts churned through my mind as I lay in the darkened room. Could I trust Bud? Might the cops come because he was a drug peddler? Would they arrest him? Me, too? Why had I lied so? Guilt, remorse and fear fought within me, as I tossed and turned, trying to go to sleep.

After a while Bud's door opened quietly.

"Carmen," he whispered. You asleep? Excuse me, but I need a drink of water."

When I didn't answer, he tiptoed across the room and went into the kitchen. I listened to the water running. What was coming next?

Through half-closed eyes, I watched him walk into the living room, carrying a half-empty glass of water. He walked over to my bed, leaned over, and said gently, "Carmen, how you doin'?"

"Just fine," I quavered. I was scared and pleased both.

"I just want you to know you can stay here as long as you want to," he said, and leaned over and patted my cheek.

"Oh, Bud, you really are the greatest! I don't know what I'd do without you."

He set the glass down on the table and sat on the edge of the bed. "Go to sleep," he said, and started to rub my back. Delicious sensations ran through me—I felt calmer yet more excited at the same time. Then he reached over gently and kissed me.

I responded. Here at last was someone who loved me and whom I could love. He was gentle and kind; he'd never hurt me and he'd look after me.

Bud took good care of me. He bought me clothes; he took me out to dinner; he paid me thoughtful little attentions. There were times during that next four months when guilt feelings almost overwhelmed me, but somehow I managed to justify my actions. After all, he did let me stay with him and I *did* owe him something more than just cooking and cleaning for him.

One night when Bud left on his usual trip to pick up heroin, remorse and guilt overcame me. I felt so down, I didn't know what to do. Then I thought of the stuff Bud had stashed away in the bathroom. He always kept some spare, so he never ran out. Boy, how I needed to get off. I fought the urge, at first, because Bud never took the stuff himself, but I kept remembering that set of works he kept for others to use.

Finally, I went to the picture frame, pulled out a bag and ran into the bathroom and pulled out the works. It was awkward trying to drill myself that first time, but I finally got the needle to work. Oh, what a wonderful feeling!

I washed the works carefully and restored them to their hiding place. When Bud got back, I was still high and I figured I'd better tell him what I'd done.

"You little fool!" he screamed. "You don't know what

you're doing! You'll wind up a no-good junkie."

I had thought he might get mad, but I hadn't realized he would be that furious. I was frightened, and I started to cry. I apologized and begged him to forgive me, and finally he simmered down a little. (Somehow I had figured that since Bud sold the stuff, he would understand my need.)

"All right, Carmen," he said. "I'll forget it this time, but don't ever let it happen again. And I'm not fooling. No junkie is going to live with me!"

For a few days, Bud acted rather cool, but I tried hard to make it up to him. I cooked his favorite dishes and polished the whole apartment. By the end of the week, we were back on our old, comfortable footing.

Then, one night, when Bud returned from his usual errand, he sat down with me and started to talk about getting arrested. He picked up the day's paper and read me a story about a carrier who'd been picked up. The carrier was a man Bud usually met in the men's room of a nearby restaurant. The newspaper story said this guy got his drugs from the Mafia. He told me about another connection, who was a Cuban.

"They're getting a lot of stuff in from Cuba these days," he said. "Well, the cops picked *him* up today. Carmen, I just have the feeling I'm going to wind up on Riker's Island again. I just don't think I could go through it again. I know —I spent three years there once."

I did what I could to reassure him, but I was scared myself, so it didn't do much good. He went to bed, still despondent.

A few nights later, he came in breathless. "The Feds are chasing me," he announced.

We sat there, waiting for the bell, or for a knock at the

door. Nothing happened. Not that night nor any of the nights that followed. But Bud got jumpier and jumpier, and he paid less and less attention to me. We had more and more arguments.

I was worried about him. I didn't want to see him in jail; I loved him. But I couldn't help worrying about *me,* also. What would happen to me, if Bud were arrested?

Of course, there came another night when he went out, and I succumbed to my urge again. But this time, I didn't tell Bud about it, and he never guessed. He was too preoccupied with his own troubles to pay much attention to me.

After that, most nights right after he left, I headed for the picture frame and the bathroom. I was lucky, until one night I found five bags behind the frame. Greediness got the better of me, and I put all five in the cooker and got off.

What a hit! All my fears, frustrations and heartaches disappeared. I was riding on cloud nine when Bud got home, later that evening.

He took one look at my nodding head and glazed smiles and that was it. Next thing I knew, I was being yanked out of my chair. He literally flung me against the wall. I didn't resist; I just slumped down and stared dully at him. I didn't even care.

"You dirty, good-for-nothing junkie," he snarled at me. "Get out of my place and don't you ever come back."

"Bud, Bud . . . Bud, please let me explain."

"No more phony excuses. I told you once, and I meant it. Out, out, out," he repeated, and pushed me toward the door and slammed it after me.

"Bud, Bud, let me in," I pleaded, and knocked on its blank surface.

The door opened slightly, and I heard Bud's grim voice, "Carmen, get out now and get out quick, before we're both sorry."

As I started to plead some more, my eyes slid down to the knob of the door. An open switchblade flicked at me.

I couldn't believe it. I continued to stand there, just dumb. I heard the words "Get going," repeated and felt the tip of the knife.

I turned and walked down the hall, out into the night. Where would I go? What would I do? I had no home. No Lulu, and now—no Bud. I had absolutely nothing.

CHAPTER • 5

I WANDERED AROUND on the subway for a couple of hours I got off at Fourth and Atlantic, the corner I had watched Lulu solicit on, many, many nights ago. . . .

I was sick, tired, bewildered. The only thing I was sure of was that I had to get off, so I could get straight. How? All my tired mind could produce was that Lulu had picked up money fast right here.

I stood by the wall, watching people walk by. A couple of times, I managed a half-hearted smile, but the hurrying men didn't give me a second glance.

"Hey, what're you doing out here?" I turned half-way around in order to identify the voice, which came from a faintly familiar face. The girl appeared to be about twenty, and I knew I had met her somewhere, but I couldn't remember where.

"Don't you remember me? We met at Bud's place," she said.

"Oh, yes. You're Nancy." She was one of those who had come by the apartment several times to buy drugs.

"Sorry, I forgot your name, but that doesn't matter. What are you doing out here?" she repeated.

"Carmen's my name," I answered. "It's a long story. . .

Bud and I had a fight and we finally agreed we weren't meant for each other. Tonight when he went out, I just packed up and left. I hated to do it, but it was best for both of us, I guess." I bowed my head, and a few tears trickled down my cheek. Inside, a part of me stood aside and marveled at my playacting, and was disgusted and ashamed at the lying and deceit. But I was too ashamed to tell her the truth.

When Nancy put her arm around my shoulder, the playacting stopped, and tears and sobs of real fear and loneliness gushed out.

"Nancy, I'm sick, I'm frightened, and I *have* to get off. The only thing I can think of to do is to pick up a man, but I just plain don't know how. And if I did land one, what would I do? Where would I go?"

"There, there," she said and patted my shoulder. "Nancy'll look after you. Don't worry. With your looks, you'll do real good. First, though, I'll show you the ropes. C'mon, I'll show you where to take a guy."

We walked down to Dean Street and stopped at a tenement in the middle of the block. There was a strong smell of urine in the hall, and as we climbed the stairs, I noticed four-letter words scribbled all over the walls. The stairs creaked and trembled under our weight and I was glad that we had no farther to go than the second floor.

A man answered Nancy's knock.

"Hugh, this is Carmen, a friend of mine," she said. "She's new in the block and I told her you'd have a room for her when she needs one. OK?"

"OK," Hugh said. I started to thank him, but he shut the door abruptly, and that was that.

I looked at Nancy questioningly, but she laughed and

said, "Don't mind Hugh. Everything is strictly business with him. And don't forget he wants the two bucks *before* you use the room."

I checked the number of the house—932—when we got back on the street. As we headed back toward the Avenue, I tried to steel myself to the idea of bringing a man—any man—to this filthy place. I felt nasty and dirty already. How could I do it?

"Nancy," I burst out. "How do you ever do it? Don't you ever feel guilty or ashamed?"

"I used to feel terrible. I wasn't brought up for this. But I found the only way to get over the guilt."

"How?"

"Always get off, before you hit the street. That high feeling can carry you through anything—any man, whoever he is. Tell you what I'll do," she added. "I live just across the street and I've got a little stuff stashed away. I can see you're sick and you need it, so c'mon, we'll go get off together."

We crossed the street and walked into a tenement that was a twin of Hugh's—the same smell, the same words. This time we had to brave the rickety stairs for three flights. We walked into a hall bathroom, and Nancy yanked a set of works out of her bra, then reached into the hem of her skirt and withdrew three bags of heroin, carefully.

"Do you always carry your works in your bra?" I asked as I watched her prepare the fix.

"That depends. Sometimes I hide it in my apartment. But once in a while the cops drop by, and if they find it here they'll bust me."

While she was talking, Nancy had removed a stocking and wrapped it around her arm. She got off and then handed me the stocking. My practice alone made it possible for me to get off quickly; I was rather proud that I managed so nicely doing it by myself, with someone else watching.

My fear vanished. It was just as Nancy had said. I wasn't afraid to go out on the street; I wasn't afraid to tackle anything or anyone!

Nancy rinsed out the works methodically and stuck them back in their storage plaçe, and we started down the hall. She stopped by another door, reached into her bra and pulled out a key.

"Good lord!" I exclaimed. "Do you keep *everything* in your bra?"

"Not quite," she said, and opened the door. "This is my place. Not much, but at least it's a bed. I live with a guy named Gene."

I looked around. She was right, it wasn't much. Just two rooms—a small kitchen and a little larger room, which held a sofa and a disheveled, unmade bed.

"If you want to put up here a while, you can have the sofa," she offered.

My thoughts flashed back to Bud's apartment: the wall-to-wall carpeting, the slip-covered furniture, the tastefully decorated bedroom, the color TV. Nancy had no TV at all. I looked queasily at the threadbare linoleum, laced with pot holes to catch an unwary heel; the sagging spring of the bed that almost touched the floor; the greasy upholstery of the sofa, most of which was coming out in worn spots here and there. Worst of all, three of us would share this shoddy room.

"Thanks, I appreciate it," I said. After all, it was better than a park bench.

She nodded, then moved briskly toward the door.

"Ready for your first trick?" she asked.

"Trick?"

"Yeah, that's what we call the men."

I was learning. I hung on every word Nancy said, as we headed back to the Avenue.

"Listen carefully," she said. "All you have to do is stand there and look like you got something to sell. You have it, so don't worry. Just give them the eye, smile, and believe me, they'll come flocking. You're clean, you're young, you're pretty. That's what they want. Go ahead. I'll be just across the street watching."

I took a deep breath as I watched her cross the street. Then I leaned up against a nearby hot dog stand, and put on what I hoped was an inviting smile.

It wasn't long—maybe five minutes—before a man stopped. He was fat and bald; he looked about fifty.

"You working tonight?" he asked.

"You bet!"

"Can we go to your place?"

"Sure. It's only two blocks away."

Inwardly I gloated, this was just too easy! The fix had rid me of my guilt and shame. It all seemed simple. I tried to make conversation with the man, as we walked along, but beyond grunting his name, he had little to say—just kept eyeing me up and down.

For a second I forgot the number of the house, then I recognized the battered brick front of 932.

I walked inside confidently. As the man followed me, I stopped and said, "My price is fifteen dollars, Bob. Business before pleasure."

He pulled out a wad, counted out a five and a ten and handed them to me silently. I tried to be casual about tucking the money into my bra, but it felt crinkly and uncomfortable. I reminded myself that it felt reassuring too.

I knocked on Hugh's door and, when he opened it, I pulled the five out and put it in his hand. He handed me back three ones, let us in and pointed toward a back room. As I stumbled down the smelly, dimly-lit hall, I was appalled at the filth in the living room opposite. It was worse than Nancy's.

Hugh got up and opened the door for me when I left. As I stepped into the hall, he slapped me familiarly.

I whirled around, and glared at him. "Get your dirty hands off me, and don't ever touch me again!" I snapped.

Hugh laughed. "Some day, Baby, you may be beggin'. Just wait and see." He shut the door and I walked on down to the street, feeling ashamed and guilty. Only the crackle of the uncomfortable bills wedged in my bra comforted me. I knew I needed another fix.

When I got back to the avenue, I looked around for Nancy, but she was nowhere to be seen. Probably she got herself a trick, I reasoned. And sure enough, a few minutes later, she came up to me.

"Nice goin'," she said. "How much'd you get?"

"Fifteen," I answered. I was soon to learn "How much'd you get?" was always the first question—as it should be. Prostitution is just for money; the money is just to support your habit; your habit makes you need the money; to get the money you have to prostitute; and the money gets you the drugs. It's a real sickening merry-go-round, but there's no way to get off.

"Good girl. Let's go get off again."

"Again? We did less than an hour ago," I said.

"Listen, Baby, remember what I told you. It's a lot easier when you're high. Remember? It's a long night, and if you're really going to hustle, you've gotta *hustle.*" She laughed at her play on words.

"Yeah," I replied. I remembered. I knew I could never go up to Hugh's again, if I wasn't high. "Let's go."

Nancy's connection lived right near her apartment, so we stopped there and we each picked up a few bags. When we reached her apartment, she had more words of wisdom for me.

"This time, we're only going to use two bags. We're going to save one for later—for the morning, maybe. You probably won't get to bed, to sleep, until five or six in the morning, and when you wake up, most likely you'll feel sick. You'll need something to get you straight. So . . . always keep something in reserve. One bag isn't really enough to help much, but don't forget, you'll pick up more money and you'll pick up more stuff. Always put at least one aside each time. By the time the night's over, I'll have at least three bags in reserve."

Here was a smart junkie! Nancy continued to talk, as she got the works out and prepared the fix. "When I first started out, I made a real pig of myself over junk. I shot up everything I got my hands on, all at once. But after I had to go out on the street sick a few times, I learned."

We got off, and as Nancy cleaned and put her works back in her bra, she told me I could hide my bag behind the baseboard. I knelt, slid the board away slightly and slipped the bag in.

We returned to the street. Nancy crossed over and I

returned to my position in front of the hot dog stand. A few minutes later, a man stopped. We went through the same routine as I had with Bob: first the money, then Hugh's, then back to the street.

By five in the morning, Nancy came over to me and said, "C'mon, let's call it a night. You've had a good first night; now it's time to turn in."

Gene was home when we got there. He was pretty much of a creep, I thought. A guy who hung out at the restaurant near the station and never did a lick of work, except once in a while to act as Nancy's pimp. I wondered aloud why she let him live with her.

"Some day you'll see the importance of a guy like Gene," she explained. "He looks out for me. Whenever I bring a guy to the apartment, Gene is right close by. Some of these guys are perverts—even nuts that try to kill you. With Gene around, all I have to do is yell for help, and he's right there. Besides, on slow nights, he sometimes drums up a little trade for me."

Next night I returned to the Avenue. In the course of the evening I met some of the other girls, plying the same trade. They came in all sizes, shapes and personalities. Some were so strung out (had such bad habits) they were willing to do anything a trick asked: perversion, whatever. I was sure glad I didn't have to submit to anything like that, **and I swore privately I'd never let myself get that far gone!**

One night, Hugh gave me a little advice. "Carmen, you're new at this game," he said. "Some night in that room, you may need me. All you have to do is yell. I'm right here, and so is ole Jack here too." Hugh pulled his shirt back and showed me the revolver tucked into his belt. I looked at the gun, then up at Hugh's face. He was dead serious. I was more than a little scared, but at the same time it was comforting to know I had a protector.

"Gee, thanks, Hugh. I appreciate your help," I said, little realizing how soon I'd be calling on him.

I got some pretty steady trade from quite a few guys, but naturally I had new ones, too. I had to take my chances. I was young and pretty, as Nancy had said, and that's what men were interested in. I had all kinds: men like Bob, divorced, widowers, bachelors, even a few college and high-school kids.

One night I wound up with a stranger who tried to manhandle me. I fought back, yelling all the time, "Get your paws off of me, you filthy slob." He was strong and I wasn't making much headway, so I screamed, "Hugh!"

I only had to scream once. The door crashed open and there was Hugh, hands on hips.

"Somethin' the matter, Carmen?"

The trick looked at Hugh as though measuring him. "Oh, no, Mister, we just had a little disagreement. I was just leaving," he said and bolted out of the door.

"Wow," I breathed with relief. "That was close. Thanks a million, Hugh."

As the weeks turned into months, only one thing worried me: It took more and more bags to get high. By now I was making about seventy-five dollars a night, but it barely satisfied my habit. When I went to sleep each night, I fought the urge to shoot the reserve I knew I'd need in the morning.

One evening, when I took my first trick up to Hugh's, I knocked on the door and there was no answer. I knocked again. Still no answer. What was going on? This was only the first trick of the evening. I got panicky and banged on the door, yelling, "Hugh, Hugh, let me in!"

A door down the hall opened. "Pipe down," a voice said. "Hugh doesn't live here any more. The cops came and got him. Scram!"

"Man, I'm gettin' outta here," the trick said and shot down the stairs.

I started to follow him, but stopped and let the fact that Hugh was gone sink in. Where did I go now? What did I do?

CHAPTER • 6

I SEARCHED FRANTICALLY for Nancy. She *had* to tell me what to do. Finally I ran her down at the restaurant near the station. Gene was there, too, as he always was.

"Nancy, Hugh's been busted," I cried.

"Yeah, I know. Tootsie told me. She was there when they took him away. They took Donna too."

"But what happened?"

"I don't really know. I guess maybe the guy Donna took up to Hugh's was a cop? Anyway, Donna was busted for pros and Hugh for operating a business illegally." Nancy's voice was sober, as she added, "This's the second time they've gotten Hugh. I sure hope he beats the rap."

"But, what am *I* gonna do now?" I wailed. "Whose place can I use?"

"Don't worry. Bernie has a pad in the same house. Only, he's on the fourth floor, and sometimes the tricks aren't too happy about climbing that far."

How glad I was I had Nancy! She'd been an addict and a prostitute for ten years. She knew all the ropes—where to go, what to do in any circumstance.

"Go introduce yourself to Bernie, before you take a trick

there," she advised. "Otherwise he may not let you in. It's Apartment 4-C."

I went down to 932 again and started up the stairs. As I passed the second floor, I thought of Hugh. What was he doing now? Where was he? I could see him sitting in a jail cell, down in the dumps, wondering what was going to happen to him. Poor Hugh; I sure wished he hadn't gotten busted.

By the time I reached the fourth floor, I was out of breath. I hoped I'd never have to bring a trick all the way up here when I was sick. I'd never make it.

I knocked on the door of 4-C. A tanned six-footer, around thirty-five, opened the door.

"Hi, can I help you?" he asked and flashed me a big smile. I breathed a sign of relief—at least he was friendly!

"My name is Carmen. Nancy said you might be able to help me out. I used to have a friend—Hugh—down on the second floor, but he's not available anymore," I explained.

"Yeah, I know Hugh. Sure, you can use my room anytime you want."

He didn't invite me in, but he was chatty, so we stood there in the doorway talking for a few minutes. The more we talked, the more he asked about *me.* He admitted freely that he was a junkie, but I lied like a trooper. Finally, I thanked him and headed back for the Avenue.

When a trick turned up, I trudged up to Bernie's. It could have been worse; his bedroom was a lot cleaner than Hugh's had been!

As the days went by, I ran into some trouble now and then. Once in a while, Bernie wouldn't be home, and, after that long trek up the stairs, I'd wonder if it was worth it. I'd have to wind up taking the trick to a local hotel and that was a lot more expensive. Also, if you ran into a pervert, you had no one to call on.

Months went by. Each night I was on the street; each morning I was sick and used up my reserve, so I had to go back. Days had no meaning; most of the time I didn't even know what day of the week it was. By now, I had absorbed everything Nancy and the other girls on the street had told me and added a few refinements of my own. I had gone about as far as I could go, just playing the street.

Then I got a chance to buy a phone list. It was worth the $150. You didn't have to stand on the street in any weather; you could just call a trick and go up to his place. None were perverts, so you could feel safe in the apartment—the list had been screened.

I worked the list for six months or more, but by that time I knew I was getting pretty strung out. These guys wanted a pretty, young chick; my habit was getting pretty bad and it was affecting my appearance. I tried, but after I was high, my judgment of how I looked wasn't too good. Once they saw me, they just didn't want me after that.

I decided I'd head back to the streets of Brooklyn. But when I did, the streets were different—a couple of cops stood on every corner. I drifted down the Avenue once, but I was afraid to stop anywhere; everywhere I looked I saw a cop. Finally, I walked into a restaurant, and there was Floyd! an old junkie I used to know.

"Where is everybody?" I asked.

"Where *you* been? They're really burning this place now. There's a cop any place you go."

"Wow!" I said. "What'll I do now? Isn't anybody around at all?"

"Most everybody's gone up to the Bronx," Floyd said,

"until it cools off around here. I'm headed that way. Wanna come along?"

"Sure, maybe we can find some action up there."

The two of us headed for the subway and then for Westchester Avenue. I was amazed at all the junkies standing around. Lots of girls were walking around, trying to pick up tricks, and they seemed to be having an easy job of it. This looked like good territory.

Floyd introduced me to a few of the fellows and girls, and it didn't take me long to find out where to take a trick. There were quite a few places on Simpson Street.

I stayed with different junkies for a couple of months. Most of the girls had an "old man" who lived with them. Some were legally married; most had a common-law relationship. Almost invariably the old man was a junkie, so the girl had to support his habit as well as her own.

I had a few close calls and sometimes I wished I had an old man. Also, ever since I had lived with Bud, I longed for a closer intimacy and warmth and security.

One early evening I walked down Westchester and a young fellow called out, "Hey, your blouse is hanging out." I was annoyed; I thought he was putting me on. I reached down, automatically; sure enough my shirttail *was* out. I turned around and looked at him. He was grinning broadly, so I walked over.

"Thanks for your help," I said.

"No trouble; no trouble at all," he replied. "How about a cigarette?"

"Thanks again," I said, took one and continued on down the avenue.

He looked kind of interesting, so I peeked back over my shoulder to see if he was following me. But instead of my trick, I saw a cop heading toward me. I panicked and ran blindly down Westchester, around a corner, then through a tenement, and out onto another side street. Panting, I stopped and looked behind—no cops in sight. I continued slowly on down the side street and then I saw my trick approaching on the other side of the street. Was he there to see if I had been caught? I had to find out.

"Boy, that was close," I said, when he got abreast of me.

"Sure was. They almost got you."

"They? Was there more than one?"

"Two more, right behind the first. I started to follow you, but the cop on the corner started following *me*, so I figured I better head some other way," he said. "You gotta place we can go to?"

"You got the money?"

"Don't worry about that," he said. So I led him up to the tiny room I'd taken for myself. When I opened the door, I was ashamed. It was as bad or worse than Nancy's. Somehow I never seemed to have the time or energy to make the bed or clean the place up a bit.

"What's your name?" he asked. "Mine's Vinnie."

"Carmen," I said shortly, and held my hand out for money. He handed me twenty dollars.

Afterwards we sat around and talked for a while. This trick really interested me; he didn't just get up and go as the others did. He made me think of Bud. He asked me about myself. He told me he was a chef at a hotel in Manhattan.

Finally, I got up reluctantly. "I've got to get going again," I told him.

"OK. I'll see you again," he said, and we walked back to the street.

Around 4 A.M. a few days later, I saw Vinnie on the street again. He invited me into the all-night restaurant for a cup of coffee, and we sat there for almost an hour and talked. He told me more about himself, and when we finally finished our coffee, he handed me a twenty dollar bill.

"Let's go," I said, ready to take him up to my room.

"Listen, Carmen, I just got off work," Vinnie said. "I'm going home to get some shut-eye. You keep the money." He put his arm around my shoulder and dropped a kiss on the top of my head. "I really feel sorry for you," he said and walked off.

It got to be kind of a habit—meeting Vinnie around 4 A.M. and having a cup of coffee. Most times, he'd give me a twenty and leave me, but one night, he invited me up to his place.

I marveled at the cleanliness. It wasn't as grand an apartment as Bud's, but it was nice, and it was immaculate. Before I left, he invited me into the bedroom, and again he gave me a twenty.

When I got ready to leave, Vinnie looked at me and said, "Carmen, why don't you stay here a while. You look dead on your feet."

"I really am," I said. "I could use some sleep. Are you sure you don't mind?"

The twenty-dollar bill crackled reassuringly in my bra and the clean bed looked so inviting I agreed. I flopped down on the bed.

Vinnie didn't touch me and in a few moments I was sound asleep. I didn't wake up for quite a while—much longer than I usually slept. Was it the clean sheets? The comfortable bed? Or the comfortable Vinnie? I didn't know. For a moment I luxuriated, then the sickness set in. I knew I had to get out, and off. . . .

Vinnie was nowhere to be seen, but as I dressed hastily, I could smell bacon and coffee. I almost made it to the door, when he appeared.

"Hey, wait a minute. How about some breakfast?"

"Sorry. I'm not feeling so hot. I've got to get out of here," I said, and bolted out of the door. I managed to make it to Westchester, find my connection and get off before I collapsed.

Next morning around four o'clock there was Vinnie again. It got so I wound up at his place to sleep four or five nights a week. It was real nice to go there; his place was always so clean compared with my dirty old dump, and he treated me with such respect and kindness. Finally, I reached the point that I'd knock off early and hang around waiting for him to finish work, hoping he'd invite me over.

Unknown to Vinnie, I'd use his bathroom to get off. Usually, I tried to wait until he went to sleep, but once in a while I managed to sneak in, while he was still up. Each time I went, he gave me a twenty. I told him he didn't have to, but he insisted, and I was so greedy for money to support my habit, I didn't argue too much.

I had a real good trade one night, so I decided to quit early. I went to my room about two and got off. I crawled into bed at last and had just fallen asleep when a knock came at the door. It must be the cops, was my first reaction.

"Who is it?" I called, fearfully.

No answer. The knock came again, this time more insistent.

I was galvanized with fright. "Who is it?" I yelled.

"Vinnie."

I leaped out of bed, looked at the clock and saw that it was almost five.

I opened the door, words of apology on my lips, but Vinnie never let me get them out. "I've been looking all over for you." he said. "Finally, I decided to try here."

He looked around the dirty room with distaste, then brought his embarrassed eyes back to me.

"Carmen, I've come to take you home. I want you to live with me. I think you need me," he said, simply.

I was feeling a little sick, and I was embarrassed and annoyed at having him catch me in this filthy pigsty.

"Look, Vinnie. I'm not looking for any husband, boyfriend, pimp—anybody to get attached to. Anybody's got the money, I'm here. Besides that, I'm an addict, and you sure don't want a dope addict for an old lady."

"Aw, don't worry about that," he said. "Carmen, I mean it. You need me and I'm discovering I need you. I got a few friends that fool around with marijuana and they're really not all that bad."

It was obvious Vinnie thought I was a novice. I needed a fix—and bad. I decided the best way to get rid of him, and to ease my guilt, was to shock him.

"Look at these arms," I said and drew up my sleeve. "See right there. That's a track; I'm a mainline junkie. Get out of here; you want no part of the likes of me."

"Carmen, I know you. You aren't all that bad," he pleaded. "You're too nice a girl to be a real junkie."

This guy was too nice to have a junkie wife, I decided. I'd have to show him.

"OK. Just sit down in that chair and I'll show you something you'll never forget," I said.

Obediently, Vinnie perched on the only chair in the

room. I walked into the bathroom, got the works and some heroin and returned to the other room. He might as well see all the gory details, I decided, and I got off, while he sat there and watched in silence. He didn't say a word the whole time.

"Now," I said, "you *know* I'm a junkie. Get out and stay away. I'm not the girl for you."

"You've just convinced me more than ever that you need me," Vinnie insisted. "Carmen, please come with me."

I offered a few more feeble arguments, then he helped me pack the few things I had in my bag and I moved in with him.

I kept on hustling in the street. Vinnie didn't like it much, but he didn't say much about it, either. Every time I got off Vinnie watched me, as though he were hypnotized. Each time I put the needle in, he grimaced.

Once, after I got off, I left the needle on the coffee table and went off to the bathroom. I was afraid he was beginning to get interested in drugs. I left the door ajar, and sure enough, soon he picked up the needle. First, he just looked at it, then he took an experimental jab at the back of his hand.

"What do you think you're doing?" I yelled at him and grabbed the needle away. "Don't you ever dare touch my works again!"

"It seems to do so much for you," he said. "Every time I watch you, I think maybe I should try it, too."

"Oh! So you want to wind up a junkie, too? OK. I'll show you just how it is," I said. "You stay here and I'll prepare you a fix and then you'll know exactly how it feels."

I picked up the works and headed for the bathroom. The only way to dissuade him was to fool him, I realized. Fleetingly, I remembered Bud. Now I knew how he'd felt when he'd caught me using a needle. I didn't want Vinnie to end up that way. He was too good a guy. I knew Vinnie was scared of needles. Maybe if I scared him badly enough, he'd steer clear of the stuff.

I left the bathroom door open so Vinnie could see me, and reached under the sink and pulled out a bag. I pretended to open it and put it in the cooker, making as much noise as I could so he would be sure I was doing something important. Then I drew some tap water into the needle.

Vinnie was still sitting where I had left him, watching the bathroom door as though he was mesmerized. I held out the needle, which he thought was filled with heroin, and said, "OK, Vinnie. You asked for it. Take off your belt and puff up your veins."

His face blanched, but he did what I said.

"All right, hold out your arm. We're going to mainline," I told him.

I jabbed the needle in, not looking for a vein or anything else. He flinched; it must have hurt like crazy, because his arm drew back involuntarily, and he gave a short moan of pain.

"Shut up and keep still. You want me to bust the needle off in your arm?" I asked.

Vinnie had good veins. I drew blood back up into the dropper, and I felt his arm tighten. I glanced at him. His eyes were glued on the needle; his face was ashen.

"Here it comes," I said. "All that rich, gooey blood!"

Vinnie looked at his arm, then at me. I thought he might faint, but he clenched his teeth and held on.

"Vinnie," I begged. "You're a fool. You don't want this. Take it from me—you're just one step away from a living hell."

He didn't say a word, but managed to nod his head at me. I shot the water and blood back into his arm, jerked the needle out and went to the bathroom to rinse it out. When I came out, Vinnie was sitting on the chair, just as I'd left him—the belt still on his arm. He didn't say a word.

Nor did I. I walked right on out the door and onto the street, and began to hustle. For the first time in a long while, I felt pretty good. I was sure I'd scared the devil out of Vinnie and he'd never want another shot.

I got home around 3 A.M. and was shocked to find Vinnie there.

"What're you doing home so early?" I asked.

"Aw, I just didn't feel like going to work," he answered. His voice was fuzzy; I looked at him carefully. Oh, my God —Vinnie was high!

"Where'd you get the stuff? What do you think you're doing? Are you crazy?"

I was beside myself with rage. Here, I thought I'd done the one good deed of my life and what did I find?

"From you," Vinnie said, and his head started to nod. He had a silly grin on his face. "It feels good, Carmen."

"Good!" I screamed. "You crazy idiot, don't give me any of that 'feels good' bit. Someday you may have to crawl on your belly to *feel good.* And how'll you like that?"

But Vinnie was too far gone to care. Somehow he'd found my reserve bags and my works, and he'd taken enough to just sit there and nod and smile and be happy. I was so mad and upset I didn't even get off myself, just crawled into bed and cried. I looked over at him and remembered the time Bonnie gave me my first marijuana —the first time I got high. I wished I was clean enough to get that innocent feeling again. Now, all I worried about was getting straight; I couldn't keep much of a high any more, because my habit was too great. Just enough to get the junk out of my veins and go out to hustle for more. Now, the only person I cared about I'd gotten into the habit!

The next evening Vinnie went to work. I was relieved; at least he wasn't going to quit his job.

He kept on at the job for three weeks and I didn't find him high again, so I went back to my old custom of bringing a girl friend or two home with me once in a while. We'd get off together and then sit around and talk. Since Nancy was my oldest friend, naturally she usually came. They would be gone by the time Vinnie came in, generally.

One night, Sarah, Nancy and I came in about 1 A.M., and there sat Vinnie watching television. His head was nodding and his eyes were glazed—he was high again!

"What are you doing home?" I asked.

"Oh, the boss let me off tonight. I wasn't feeling too good," he said and looked at Nancy and Sarah. I knew he was lying. All I could do was pray that he hadn't been fired.

I hesitated before I took the girls into the bathroom for a fix. Ever since Vinnie had gotten high, I'd tried not to let him see me do it. But I was tired, and the two girls had come solely to get off, so I led the way.

When we came out, we went into the living room and sat down with Vinnie. He wasn't very communicative, just gave me a dirty look and kept on staring at the TV.

Sarah had told me sometime ago that Nancy was a Lesbian, but Nan had never tried anything with me, and I still considered her my best friend. I trusted Nancy, and she knew it.

"Guess we better get goin'," Nancy finally said uneasily, and Sarah nodded.

As soon as the front door shut after them, Vinnie bolted out of his chair.

"You dirty little Lesbian," he yelled. "What do you mean, letting that tramp in here?"

Then he leaped at me, arm upraised. I saw that he held a dog chain in his hand and I tried to duck, but the chain caught me across the side.

"Vinnie, Vinnie," I screamed, "I'm no Lesbian. You know that. I hate them as much as you do. Nancy isn't. . . . "

The chain whistled through the air again and this time struck my back. I cowered on the floor, covering my face with my hands as best I could, as the chain slashed at me once more. I was crying from pain and fear and finally Vinnie stopped. He was panting hard.

Slowly, I looked through parted fingers and saw the chain lying limply in his hand. I reached over and put an arm around his legs.

"Vinnie, believe me, I'm no Lesbian, and I never will be. I'm your woman, and that's it," I said reassuringly.

I started to struggle to my feet and Vinnie leaned over and helped me up.

"I'm sorry, Carmen," he said, "I never should have hit you, but I am insanely jealous of you, and the thought of you with someone else—even a girl—drove me out of my skull." (Obviously, being a prostitute didn't count!)

I stayed in the rest of the night. I had to convince Vinnie I *was* his woman. I knew I couldn't leave him as I had my family and Bud. I'd only wind up on the street and I certainly didn't want that.

We got up late in the afternoon and I waited for Vinnie to get ready for work, but he kept stalling. I needed to get off in the worst way, but I was determined I wouldn't do it while he was around. He was in deep enough already, without me encouraging him.

"Vinnie, you better get going or you'll be late for work," I urged. I was getting sicker by the minute.

Still he kept stalling.

"*Will* you get out of here and get to work?" I yelled, finally. And then I held my breath; I didn't want another beating and now I could never be totally sure again.

"I lost my job."

"Well, don't you think you ought to look for another?" I said as calmly as I could.

"No," was his only response.

I just couldn't wait any longer. I ran into the bathroom and prepared a fix. Just as I was about to put the needle in my arm, Vinnie walked in.

"I want to get off, too," he said and stared at the needle.

"Vinnie, stay away from this stuff. It'll kill you," I pleaded, but I knew I was fighting a losing game.

He reached over and grabbed the needle from my hand. "Gimme that."

"All right," I said. "All right. Take it easy, you can get off with me. Just give me the needle back."

He handed it over and I got off first, then I drilled Vinnie. He felt it right away and started to nod. I was too old a hand to have it affect me as much, so I headed out to the street.

When I came back to the apartment after a couple of tricks, Vinnie was waiting for me. There was no reserve left in the apartment and he knew I'd have to make a connection. We had another big argument and, again, I gave in. We got off together, and I went back to the street.

A few hours later I returned to the apartment just as Vinnie walked out of the bedroom. He started to say something, then thought better of it, and slumped down on the sofa.

In a few moments, Sarah followed him out of the bedroom.

"What's going on here?" I yelled, looking first at one, then the other.

"I was a little tired," Sarah faltered. "And Vinnie . . . Vinnie said I could rest here a while."

I tried to believe her; I *wanted* to believe her, but as I looked at Vinnie, head down, eyes riveted on the floor, I knew she was lying.

"Get out of my house, you little tramp," I told her. "And don't you ever come back again."

As Sarah walked out of the door, Vinnie headed for the kitchen. I followed him out.

"All right, Buster, just what goes on here?"

"None of your business," he snapped.

I reached out to slap his face, but he caught my arm and slung me around. He slapped me across the face several times.

"Listen, woman," he said and slapped me again. "No one hits Vinnie and gets away with it. *No one!* Understand?"

There was no sense trying to fight back—I'd wind up black and blue or worse. What irony! He accused me of Lesbianism and then beat me because *he* played around with a friend of mine.

I didn't say anything, just turned and walked into the bathroom. Vinnie walked in right after me.

"Give me that needle," he commanded. And this time *he* got off first. From that time on, Vinnie always got off first. It made no difference how sick I was, how much money I'd earned, or that I was supporting *his* habit—he got off first.

It wasn't long before Vinnie was completely hooked. He didn't even try to find a job, just hung out on the street and "looked after me." Naturally he didn't want any screwball killing me. Who would support his habit then?

One night I had a good trade and, as I handed over my earnings to Vinnie, as I always did, he beamed. He was high, nodding and acting silly.

He reached out and hugged me. "Carmen, Baby, I love you," he said so passersby could hear.

I took a good look at this crazy, jumping junkie. Love? I didn't really know what love was.

CHAPTER • 7

ONE EVENING I'd been out on the street for quite a while, but not a single trick showed up. The driving rain was keeping most people indoors, and only a few cars whished by. My nose was running and my skin itched—partly because I was getting sicker by the minute, partly because of the rain and wind.

Occasionally a car stopped and the driver offered me a lift, but I refused. Too many girls had been killed or hurt by perverts offering rides. Besides, the plain clothes narcotic men used the same ploy to trap us.

Each car that stopped made me more nervous. I was positive something awful was going to happen. I watched two men in a tan coupé cruise by on the other side of the street. They made a U-turn and pulled up beside me. One rolled his window down and asked, "Hey, what're you doin' out in all this rain walking along and stopping all the cars?"

"Stopping all the cars?" I was indignant.

"Aw, you got a cold," he said sympathetically, as I wiped my dribbling nose.

"Yes," I said.

"Use junk?" he asked quickly.

"Me? Use junk? Are you crazy? I'm no junkie, Mister. Beat it, before I call the cops."

"We are the cops," he said and jumped out of the car. He grabbed my arm and searched through my pockets.

"All right, sister, into the car," he commanded. He shoved me into the back seat. "So, you're not on stuff? Well, maybe not, but no one's out on a night like tonight for any *good* reason—it must be pros. We'll take you into the precinct, just to be safe. If nothing else, we can bust you for loitering."

"What's your name?" the one in the back asked, as the driver pulled away from the curb.

"Carmen," I replied. I'd heard enough about being busted, booked and jailed from other junkies. That was one of their favorite topics of conversation. I was scared to give a false name.

"Where do you live?"

"Longfellow Street."

"Age?"

"Twenty-one."

All the way to the station house he kept asking me the same questions over and over again, hoping to trip me up.

I was scared witless; the thought of going to jail threw me. The pressure was too much—I started to cry, and, between sobs, blurted out: "All right, I'll tell you the truth. I am on stuff, but I'm trying to kick it by myself. See how sick I am? Honest, I don't want to live this life anymore."

I pleaded for mercy. I told them about my horrible parents, about Vinnie making me hustle for him. If only I could go free, I'd reform, I said.

"Sorry, Sweetheart," the driver drawled. "You're going to have to tell that to the judge."

"Please, please let me go; I'll never hustle again," I begged. I got nothing in return but shrugs from the two policemen.

Finally, I gave up. As I settled back in the seat, I began to realize that the trip to the precinct was taking an awfully long time. We should have reached there long before now. Just as I opened my mouth to ask what was going on, the driver turned off the thoroughfare onto a dark, side street and pulled up under a tree. What *was* going on? No precinct house was on *this* street—it was pitch black, not even a street light.

"Hey, what are we doing here?"

"Well, Joe," the cop in the back spoke up. "Shall we bring her in or shall we let her go?"

Hope surged through me—maybe they'd let me go. I reached over and tugged at his lapel.

"Oh, please, *please* let me go. I swear I'll never do wrong again."

"OK, Dearie," he said, and looked right into my eyes. "But it's going to cost you something."

"But . . . but, I've no money," I started to protest, and then I realized it wasn't money they wanted.

"All right," I said. "Just promise you won't bust me."

"We promise, don't we, Joe?" he laughed.

Some time later I got out of the car and staggered down the wet street. The police car pulled off and I was left—where? I hadn't the faintest idea where I was, the upper reaches of the Bronx, I guessed.

Sometime later—it seemed like years to me—I came to a lighted street. A few cars passed, and I waved frantically, trying to hitch a ride. I was too exhausted and scared to worry about perverts by this time. Nothing could be worse than what I'd just gone through. But none stopped. Finally,

I came to a traffic light, A car was waiting for the light to change.

I knocked on the window. "Mister, my car stalled about three blocks away. I have to get back to my family. Are you going down to the Bronx? Or can you give me a lift part way?"

The man stared at my disheveled appearance and frowned. He started to shake his head, then smiled suddenly and opened the door.

"OK, lady, get in," he said. "You look like a drowned rat, but who wouldn't on a night like this?"

"Thanks, thanks a million," I gasped, as I sank down on the seat beside him. "I know I must be a mess, but that rain and wind sure can beat you up."

He didn't seem inclined to talk, which didn't make me unhappy. I was sore and sick and disgusted. Law and order? The next time I heard that expression, I'd sure tell someone off! I needed a fix, like I'd never needed one before.

He let me off at Westchester and Simpson. Vinnie spotted me, as I stepped out of the car, and came tearing up. He interrupted my thanks to the kind motorist: "Carmen, where *have* you been?" His tone was suspicious. "I saw those two cops pick you up, and I went on down to the station house, but you weren't there."

"Don't question me!" I snapped. "I need a fix bad."

"C'mon," he said reassuringly, "I've got something back in the apartment."

"Where'd you get it?"

"Never mind," he replied. "Keep your mouth shut and keep on walking." Then he added, "But, *how* did you get out of it? And where you been?"

"I sold my way out," I said shortly. "And hitched a ride

back from that godforsaken place those cops took me."

"Wow, where did you get all that?" I asked as Vinnie pulled five bags out of his sock, back at the apartment. This would really put some strength back in me!

"I had to rap a guy over the head to get it."

"You mean you actually mugged someone?" I asked incredulously. I couldn't imagine Vinnie being that tough, except with me.

"Yeah. Walt showed me how. There's really nothing to it." As he prepared the fix, Vinnie continued, "All you gotta do is put a knife to his throat. You've no idea how easy it is. As Walt said, 'Either they shut up, or we slice their heads off.' We got fifty bucks off this old geezer, and Wally gave me half."

As usual, Vinnie got off first, then me. By that time I didn't care much where the money had come from, as long as we had the stuff. Vinnie continued to talk; he was obviously very proud of this new achievement of his.

"You should have heard that old buzzard plead for mercy, Carmen. It was really funny. For a second or two I thought I might slice him up a bit, just for the fun of it, but I figured if he was just scared—not hurt—we might be able to hit him again. He started to yell a little, so Walt tapped him on the head, and we beat it. After he split with me, I went and got five bags."

By the time he finished the story, my head was nodding, and we went to bed.

When we got up, Vinnie said, "I know another place where we can get money. C'mon, let's get outta here."

Out on the street, he explained: "I learned this gimmick

from Paul. You read the obituary columns every night for a while. Usually, the time of the funeral is given, as well as the name and address of the dead person. Once you find that out, it's easy as pie. You just go to the address while the funeral is on and pick up whatever you can."

"But, Vinnie," I protested, "I almost got busted tonight. Sure as anything, we can get busted for a job like this!"

"Aw, this is a natural. Paul says folks don't want to hang around the apartment or house when someone dies. That makes sense, doesn't it? If the old man kicks the bucket, then the old lady stays with a son or daughter for a while, and vice versa. She doesn't want to be reminded all the time—see?"

It made sense all right, and it sounded easy, too. But, robbery? I wasn't so sure. I got on the subway with Vinnie, still uncertain. But by the time we got off at the stop he'd picked, I decided it was worth a try.

"It's only about three blocks from here," Vinnie said. "Watch the street numbers." He had the obit in his hand.

"There it is," I cried. "That's the number in the paper."

It was a tall, fairly well-kept apartment house, and my fears returned as we walked into the lobby.

"What do we do now?" I asked.

"See if anyone's home."

"How?"

"Just knock on the door, stupid. Now listen, if someone *does* answer the door, I'll ask for the Barnes. We're looking for them—friends of ours who just moved into the apartment house. I thought this was the right apartment. I'll apologize. 'So sorry,' and all that—and we'll just walk right on out of the building."

I had to hand it to Vinnie. He had figured out all the angles. If this worked, maybe I wouldn't have to hustle anymore.

Vinnie looked at the names in the foyer. "Second floor," he whispered.

My heart was pounding as we climbed the stairs. Vinnie looked to the right, then motioned to a door on the left.

"That's it."

I held my breath, while Vinnie knocked. No answer. He knocked again. No answer. He knocked a third time, louder. Again no answer.

"Just like I told you—no one's there," he grinned. Then he headed back down the stairs.

"Where are we going?" I whispered, as I scurried after him.

"Outside, up the fire escape."

Vinnie shoved a garbage can under the fire escape, leaped up on it, grabbed the ladder and pulled it down. He held out a hand and pulled me up after him.

"Sssh," he said, as we tiptoed up the fire escape. By the time we reached the apartment window, he had a long, black metal crowbar in his hand. He slid the crowbar underneath the window and pushed down hard. A small thud, and then the bottom of the window inched up. Vinnie stuck the crowbar into his pants, slid the window all the way up and crawled in. I followed.

"All right," Vinnie ordered. "First thing you look for is money and jewelry."

I was afraid to move by myself, so I trailed him into the bedroom. Vinnie grabbed some jewelry lying on top of the dresser, and stuffed it into his pocket. Then he motioned to the drawers, and he started to ransack the bed, upending the mattress and boxspring. I found nothing in the drawers but clothes, and moved on to the closet. I wasn't doing too well in there, until Vinnie joined me; he found thirty dollars in an old shoe box.

We couldn't find any more money or jewelry, so Vinnie lifted a small portable television set out onto the fire escape. He took one more look around the room, grabbed a transistor radio and muttered, "C'mon, we better get outta here."

He had one leg over the sill and I was right behind him, when we heard someone at the door. There was a loud bang and the apartment door flew open.

"Hold it, or we shoot," a voice barked. I froze as Vinnie whirled around. Two plain clothesmen stood behind us, with drawn guns. They looked tough. I threw up my hands and so did Vinnie.

"All right. Up against the wall, face flat!"

We both turned to the wall, obediently. I didn't move fast enough to suit them, and a cop's hand slammed me against the wall. They frisked us thoroughly and naturally found the jewelry, money and crowbar on Vinnie. Both cops were old hands at this game. One pulled a knife from Vinnie's boot while the other reached into my bra and pulled out my set of works. (I had stuck them in, as we left the apartment, hoping Vinnie and I could get off before we returned.)

I was scared; they'd bust me for sure.

"All right, cut out the waterworks, sister," one of the cops said. "We're taking you both in. Save the tears for the judge."

He pulled my arms behind me and I felt the handcuffs snap on. The click was very loud in the quiet room. The cuffs were very tight; they hurt and I felt like a convict, already.

Another click—Vinnie's arms were bound this time. Then they half-pushed us out the door, downstairs and into the police car.

We reached the station house, and they shoved us up to the desk.

"We picked these two kids up in an apartment. Book them on burglary, breaking and entering, possession of works. . . ." The cop's voice droned on as he recited the charges to the desk sergeant. I lost track; it seemed like an endless list—enough to get a hundred years each.

The sergeant jotted all the information down, then began to question Vinnie and me: name, address, phone, parents, etc. It looked hopeless; I told the truth.

After an endless time, a cop led me into a back room and I saw a long row of cells. He opened one of the doors and pushed me inside. The door clanged shut; the policeman locked me in and walked back the way he had come.

I looked around the cell. It was much worse than the Youth House—just a kind of board for a bed, slab walls and no bathroom. Suddenly I realized—no window. Way down the hall, I could see a few rays of light coming in; that was the nearest window. This was truly a cage, and I felt as helpless as a bird locked in.

I realized I'd never get out. My frightened thoughts went round and round. Foremost was the stark fact that if I didn't get out of here quick, I was going to be awfully sick. I wasn't sure I could go through the hell of kicking cold turkey.

Maybe the cop would let me out? I banged on the door and yelled. No answer. I rattled the door as hard as I could and yelled, "Help, let me out of here."

The door at the end of the cell row opened and the cop who had brought me in walked deliberately over to my cell and glared in at me.

"Shut that loud mouth of yours, or I might come in and kick those pretty teeth out," he said quietly.

"Please, mister," I pleaded. "All I want to know is when do I get out of here?"

He just stared at me and didn't answer.

"Please, please, give me some idea."

"Sister, that's not my job. I'm a cop, not the judge. It's for him to say, not me," he said and turned to walk away.

"They'll probably pick you up in the morning and take you down to Centre Street," he threw over his shoulder as he opened the door into the other room again. "And cut out that yelling, or I'll be calling the morgue for your dead body." The door slammed shut.

I sat on the hard bed and stared at the wall. I was getting sicker by the minute. My head was spinning and my stomach felt as if it were full of gravel. Oh, if only I had a fix! I tried to sleep, but wound up tossing, turning, writhing. Finally I got up and looked down the hall at the window. It was getting light outside.

I thought I could hear cars outside. It must be about 6 A.M., I decided. I watched to see if anyone was coming to let me out, but no one appeared. The murmur of voices came through the door at the end of the hall, but that was all.

Finally, when I thought I could bear it no longer, the door opened and a policeman walked to my cell and unlocked it.

"OK," he said. "Come on, we're taking you to Centre Street to be arraigned."

He led me through corridors and out the back door to

a green van. Vinnie was just climbing in the back door.

"Vinnie! You all right?" I yelled.

"Shut up. No talking among prisoners," the cop said, and took me to the side door of the van. I climbed in—far, far away from Vinnie, clear at the end—the door slammed shut and we drove off. When we reached headquarters, we backed into an alleyway of sorts, the truck stopped and a cop opened the doors.

I watched Vinnie and the other men prisoners tumble out and disappear into a nearby door. A cop led me into the building and I had my picture taken, then up four floors in an elevator, down the hall and through another door—to more cells. Again, a door was opened; I stepped in, and it was locked.

I didn't have to stay there long—just long enough to get real sick. I threw up all over the place. No one came to clean it up, but I was so sick, I didn't care. Just as I dragged myself over to the bed, another cop appeared and led me downstairs to a great big cell. The minute I saw it, I recognized the bull pen I'd heard of so many times. It's where they keep all the girls who are waiting to be arraigned. The bull pen is behind a courtroom; you wait there until you're called to appear before the judge.

By the time I was taken before the judge, I was so sick I hardly knew what was going on. A lot of people were talking, but none of it made sense to me. All I wanted to do was get out of there.

That afternoon a bunch of us girls was taken to the Womens' House of Detention. What a place! We filed through a gate, one by one, waiting until each one's name was called out. Then we were taken to another room, made to take a shower and were examined by a woman doctor.

The doctor was very nice. She saw how I was suffering, and apologized for hurting me.

"I'm sorry, but I have to check you thoroughly," she said. "You're a drug addict, aren't you?"

"Yes," I replied.

"Hang on for just a few minutes more and I'll give you a shot of methadone. That'll help you get straight, so you won't feel quite so sick."

Peace! I thought. It can't really be true. Here I am a prisoner; I've done wrong. Actually I deserve the whole book thrown at me and here was this kind doctor offering to give me something to make me feel better. Life wasn't *all* bad.

"I sure do appreciate that," I said and held on until she finished the examination. She scribbled a few notes on a pad, then filled a needle with a solution from a cabinet and came back to me.

I held out my arm, waiting for her to mainline me. But she laughed.

"Sorry, but this gets injected in a different spot. Roll over, please."

I did as she said, felt the needle in my rear end, and in a few minutes, started feeling better.

"Here," said the doctor. "Here are some clothes, put them on and sit over there until I've checked a few more girls, and then you can all go up together and get a little rest."

I got dressed and waited on a bench until about another half-dozen girls were through. We were led down the hall and up to the second floor. We passed through several locked doors, which the matron unlocked and relocked each time, until we came to a long cell row. The matron motioned me to an empty cell and I stepped in; another girl followed. The door swung shut and the matron locked it.

"My name's Bessie. What's yours?"

"Carmen."

We both looked around the cell, cautiously. I could see it was a lot better than the precinct house; it had bunk beds and a toilet. We eyed each other warily, then Bessie spoke again.

"What'd you get busted for?"

"Burglary, possession of works, and. . . . I don't know what all else. Quite a lot, I think. What about you?"

"Signing bad checks—for the third time," she said resignedly.

The two of us sat down on the bottom bunk and compared notes on families, friends and whatnot. I asked Bessie if she had any idea what might happen to me.

"They'll probably take you to court in a few days," she said. "Then they'll either convict you or set you free."

"Convict you. . . ." First the handcuffs, now this. I knew I was going to wind up a convict. I could picture black and white stripes and a chain gang.

"How much time do you think I'll get?"

"Hard to say. Maybe fifteen days, maybe thirty, maybe ninety. Depends on the judge. If he gets up on the wrong side of the bed or has a fight with his wife before breakfast, he may throw the book at you. If he's in a mellow mood, he may let you off. It's all in the breaks."

By that time I was exhausted as well as discouraged. I climbed up into the top bunk, stretched out and fell sound asleep almost immediately. A scream awakened me. I started to leap out of bed, forgetting I was in the top bunk, and almost broke my neck, but I managed to twist around so I landed upright. Bessie was standing at the cell door, watching the excitement. Smoke was pouring out of one of the cells. Groggy with sleep, my first thought was to run, but then I realized I couldn't, so I stood with my roommate and watched matrons try to extinguish the blaze. One of them opened the door and led a girl out, choking and screaming.

"Wow! What in the world was that all about?" I asked Bessie.

"That girl has *really* been sick. When she first came, she could hardly walk. Ever since she got here, she's been complaining and yelling about not getting enough methadone. Poor kid, she keeps yelling she's gonna die. I suppose she's scared out of her wits at kicking cold turkey. Very few of the girls who come in here have ever kicked cold before. My guess would be she burned her mattress to get attention—and maybe another shot of methadone if she can work it."

I watched the two matrons lead the girl away.

"Where will they take her? Solitary confinement?" I asked Bessie.

"To the hospital, to intensive care," she replied.

Next day, I felt much better. I was getting a dolly every so often, and taking that pill was a lot easier than having a shot. It worked, too; I was so relieved not to have to kick cold turkey!

The day after, I was arraigned. The charges made quite an impressive list—so impressive, I thought that I was real lucky to get only ninety days.

I was allowed to remain at "The House of D," instead of going to Bedford Village. I'd heard that Bedford was a lot better, but I was getting used to where I was and felt glad I didn't have to move again.

Each day, I swore I'd never go back to drugs, and as each day passed, I felt better and better. I decided I'd give Vinnie up—maybe even go back to Jersey, live at home and get myself a regular job as a secretary or a beautician.

My stay in the House wasn't too bad; the worst part of prison life is facing up to the fact that you have no privileges at all. There isn't much to do and the days drag by slowly, each *one* seeming like *three.* I heard that some girls were put in *lock*, solitary confinement, and that some were beaten, but I never saw any of that. We had certain cleaning duties, and we were taught to sew and to work in ceramics. There was a big room where we could play records and sit around and talk; but when you're in a place with people you'd rather not be with, doing things you don't want to do, hearing the same things day after day, playing records or chatting isn't my idea of having a good time. Not too many girls used the big room.

Rumors ran wild in the place. At various times I was told of Lesbians being put in lock and girls stealing silver and being put in lock. Stealing silver was one way to create a little excitement. Some of the girls did it, just for kicks. They had a silver count in the dining room and kitchen from time to time. Usually we just had spoons—no knives ever, that I remember—sometimes forks. Sometimes at supper time, a fork or spoon would be missing. We ate in shifts and the dishwashers would report. A bell would ring and everyone out of her cell would have to report. A search of each cell would be made. I don't remember a time the missing silver didn't turn up. As I said, the girls did it just to create a little excitement—a diversion from the twenty-four-hour dullness of prison life.

Sometimes those girls were put in lock. But, I never got in too much of a sweat over them, because you were allowed to read and knit in lock, and sympathetic cellmates often brought cigarettes.

There were, of course, Lesbians there, as in all prisons. One matron was very nice to me and I liked her. Once she even brought me a cake. We kidded around quite a lot and she was a pleasant woman. Then, one day, someone told me she'd been mixed up in a deal with another girl and that she was a Lesbian, too, so after that I had nothing more to do with her.

Somehow, I got through the ninety days. The matron told me I could leave next day, and that night I hardly slept. I was up before the six o'clock breakfast bell, so excited I couldn't eat.

It was ten o'clock before the matron released me from my cell. She took me downstairs in the elevator—the first time I'd ever ridden in it—and checked me out. Another matron led me through the last locked door. When she unlocked it, I drew a deep breath. I was free!

As I walked out the door, gulping in the fresh air, I heard the matron say, mockingly, "See you later."

I whirled around; I couldn't believe my ears.

"Baby, you'll never see *me* again!" I said, and I meant it. Ninety days had gotten me off drugs and I wasn't about to go back.

The matron gave me a small salute and just grinned back. She had a reason to grin, I found out later. Eighty percent of the time she was right—they did come back.

CHAPTER • 8

AS SOON AS I got back on the block, I discovered that Vinnie had gotten ninety days, too. I looked around for him. I wanted to tell him I was finished with drugs, that I was clean and I was going to stay that way. I'd get a job; maybe he could get one, too, and we'd start a new life.

Finally, I spotted him down the block. "Vinnie!" I yelled, and ran up and threw my arms around him.

"Hi, Baby. Some ordeal, wasn't it?" and he scratched his nose.

I drew back and took a good look at him. His eyes were glassy and his nose twitched. He was high!

"Oh, Vinnie," I cried. "How could you get off so soon? Here I had all these plans. . . ."

"Yeah, man, and it sure feels good," he interrupted. "I can get you some quick. C'mon."

"Wait, Vinnie, wait," I said. "I'm not going back to drugs. I've had it. I'm going straight. I'd hoped . . . well, never mind that. It's too late now."

"Aw, c'mon, Baby. Don't be like that. Aren't you glad to see your ole man?" He reached out to embrace me.

"Get away, you lousy junkie," I told him. "Don't you touch me. I don't want junk and I want no part of junkies."

He reached out again and I slapped him full force across the face. Then I cringed, waiting for him to slap me silly. But he just put his hand up to his cheek, gave me that idiotic grin and repeated. "Man, I feel sure good!"

Hell raged within me. I knew I should walk away, but I also knew how Vinnie felt—and I envied him. Free from drugs for three months, this first high was *really* a high. I'd been told that enough times, and I could feel the craving returning. I started away, then turned and looked at Vinnie once more.

He put his hand out and smiled again. Somehow, that crazy, lopsided smile knocked my good intentions sky-high. I put my hand in his, and said, "OK, let's go."

We hadn't gone far before we ran into two junkies, Fred and Jerry.

"Good to see you back," Jerry said. "We're on our way to get off. We've got a couple of extra bags, come on along."

(Junkies are a pretty sadistic lot. Each wants to drag others into his own particular hell, so, as a rule, it's no problem for a junkie fresh out of jail to get a shot. The law of the junkie jungle seems to be: the first shot free, the rest you pay for—a mighty high price in every way.)

I left Vinnie standing on the corner and went along with them. He was still standing there, smiling and nodding when I came back.

"C'mon, let's go up the apartment," he said.

"How'd you hang on to it?" I asked. "Still the same dump?"

"Yep. Mom kept up the rent while I was in stir. Her brother's been staying there the past month or so. He just moved out this morning."

When Vinnie opened the door, I walked in and looked around curiously. Three months is a long time. The dump I remembered no longer existed. This apartment was sparkling clean. The walls had been painted, the floors scrubbed and waxed.

"What happened?" I asked Vinnie. "I don't remember *this!*"

"My uncle's a bug on cleanliness," Vinnie sounded embarrassed. "He painted and cleaned it up some, I guess."

It was nice to be able to relax in this neat, attractive apartment instead of the slovenly mess we'd left. We spent the afternoon there, talking about our jail experiences. When night came, I headed for the streets. Neither of us had a cent.

Business was better than it had been three months ago. I wondered if it was because I was clean and my hair and clothes were neat? There were a lot of new girls on the block—teen-agers. Some looked no older than fourteen or fifteen. The older tricks seemed to go for their youth.

As I stood on the corner, I watched these kids. They were hooked and hooked bad, most of them. Will these girls be drug addicts the rest of their lives? I wondered. I hadn't been much older, four years ago, when I'd hit the street, and now here I was—off the stuff for three months and clean—out hustling again to support my habit.

"Oh, God," I prayed silently. "Is this all life is meant to be? Just a vicious merry-go-round? Surely, somewhere there must be something more—for me and for these kids?"

"Hey, you, get outta here," a voice interrupted my thoughts. "This is *my* corner."

"Me?" I tried to pull myself together. "I beg your pardon. You speaking to me?"

"You bet I am." The girl who spoke was one of the teen-agers, a tall, good-looking blonde. "Get off my corner and do your hustling somewhere else."

"Baby, you're all wet," I replied. "I been around a long time and nobody's got permanent rights to any corner."

"Times change," the girl snarled. "You haven't been around lately."

She walked up to within six inches of me. "Now, scram, you tramp."

No little jerk was going to order *me* around. I was really mad by now. "Make me!" I yelled at her.

Her hand flashed out; I tried to duck, but I wasn't fast enough. I felt a searing pain across my whole face. She had slashed my cheek.

I stumbled back against the wall and saw the razor blade in her hand. My fingers traced the gash that ran down my face. The blood gushed out so I could hardly see, and the pain blinded me.

The girl eyed me, arm poised, ready to slash again.

Despite the pain and the blood, I lunged at her; I went completely berserk. My attack obviously surprised her. She fell, and I yanked the blade from her hand and slashed wildly at her. She tried to protect her face, but I hacked at her fingers until she pulled them back. All of my frustrations were bent on maiming this girl. It seemed to me that if I could kill her, somehow everything would work out. I slashed away, oblivious to her cries and to those of passersby.

Finally, a firm hand on my shoulder tugged me off. The rage let up enough for me to hear a voice, crying, "Carmen, Carmen, stop it. You're killing her!" It was Ed, one of my tricks.

"I want to kill her," I said savagely, as he pulled me to

my feet. "Look, look what she did to me!"

There was blood all over. The cut on my face was still gushing out and my clothes were soaked from it. The sidewalk looked like the Red Sea—from the girl's blood as well as my own.

A siren wailed in the distance.

"Quick, let's get out of here, Carmen," Ed said, and he started to drag me through the crowd that had gathered.

People slapped me on the back as they made a path for us. "Nice job, Carmen," someone shouted. "She was no good. She had it comin'."

I was still furious; I still wanted to kill the girl. Obviously, I wasn't the only girl she'd made trouble for. I had the crowd's approval. It was a heady feeling. If I kill her, would they give me a crown?

I tried to wriggle free, but Ed's grip was firm. He shoved me into his car, just as three police cars, with lights flashing and sirens wailing, pulled up at the corner.

"I've got to get you to the hospital fast, before you bleed to death," he said, as he pulled away from the curb. "Here, take this handkerchief and see if you can stop some of the blood."

I mopped at the cut ineffectually; the blood continued to pour out. I was getting pretty weak by the time we pulled up at the emergency entrance of the hospital. An attendant helped Ed get me out of the car and into the emergency room. The nurse there took one look at me and called for a doctor.

"Girl, you're lucky that slash wasn't two inches lower. Your head would have been lopped off," the doctor said, as he stitched my cheek.

Another nurse stuck her head in the door. "A couple of

police officers want a word with that girl, when you've finished," she said to the doctor.

"What happened to you? A dog bite you?" one of the waiting cops asked, as a nurse helped me into the anteroom.

"*Very* funny," I snapped.

"Well, what *really* happened?"

I told them everything that had happened—except why I was on the corner. I had no desire to go back to that hell hole again and, if the cops pushed me, I'd plead the Fifth Amendment.

The officers took down everything I said. "What's the other girl's name?" one asked.

"I don't even know."

"Come on, now. . . ." A nurse interrupted him. "The ambulance just brought in another girl who's been cut up."

One of the cops followed the nurse out of the room. The other one and I sat, staring at the walls. He hadn't much to say, and I hurt too much to talk.

Finally, the first cop returned, scratching his jaw. He cocked his head at me and said, "Well, looks like you girls really were mad at each other, huh?"

"You bet I was mad. Wouldn't you be, if somebody just jumped on you, right out of the blue?"

"Yeah, I guess so," he said thoughtfully. "That other kid—Lynn Wilson's her name—she's really in bad shape. The doctor's just about got to sew her whole face back together."

"You're lucky, though," he continued. "She's not going to press charges. You can go."

Ed was waiting for me and he drove me back to my apartment. Vinnie was there, wanting to hear all about the fight, but I cut him short. The pain was killing me and I needed a fix worse than I ever had in my life. Thank goodness he'd had enough sense to scare up some stuff while I was at the hospital. Once I got off, the pain lessened and I told him everything that had happened.

The next night, I was back on the corner. I looked around for Lynn. If she got smart with me again, I was prepared. Vinnie had given me one of his switchblade knives. He told me to keep it in my boot.

"If you have to use it at all, you have to use it quick," he told me.

I slid the knife in, open. If I needed it that fast, I wanted to be ready. I'd stumbled a little when I left the apartment. The knife made walking awkward, but when I got to the corner I reversed the knife, and with the blade pointed upward, I soon got used to it.

Lynn was nowhere to be seen, though, and the knife remained in my boot that night.

Not long afterwards, I was glad I had it. A trick I'd seen with some of the other girls picked me up and took me to Hunts Point. When the car stopped, I held out my hand for the money.

"I'm not gonna' pay," he snarled, and lunged at me. I twisted the door handle until the latch opened, then grabbed for the knife with my free hand. The trick had hold of the back of my jacket, but when he saw that knife come out of my boot, he let go fast. I jumped out of the car and ran down the street.

I was flushed with triumph. At last somebody was afraid of me! Lynn certainly was, and now I'd made this trick say "uncle." If only I could scare the cops and Vinnie, I thought wryly, I'd have it made!

The bandage on my face didn't seem to hurt business much. Once some of my old tricks found out I was out of jail, they came back, and I added quite a few new ones, who became regulars. Since my release from jail, I had tried to keep myself clean and neat and it seemed to work wonders. It didn't last long.

As the weeks dragged into months, I got more and more strung out again. Some days I was so sick, I hoped I'd get arrested, or even killed. Death looked like about the only way out. It took an awful lot to give me even a mild high now.

One night, as I headed for my connection, a girl told me he'd been arrested. I headed for another pusher I knew on 169th Street, only to learn she'd been busted too. It was pretty discouraging, but I decided I'd try just one more place. That guy was in jail too. It was almost too much to bear.

My mind was tired; my body cried out for a fix. What was I to do? Wearily, I looked around; maybe a cop'd pick me up and that would be that. Just my luck—no cop in sight. I knew I couldn't go on this way, but I couldn't think of anything or anyone that could help me. Then I thought of Bud. Maybe, for old time's sake, he'd sell me some? Maybe. . . . It was my only chance; I headed for Brooklyn.

On the way over, my mind went around in circles. By the time I reached his stop, I'd halfway convinced myself Bud might take me back. I was fed up with Vinnie using me, and the thought of Bud's clean, attractive apartment and the consideration he'd shown me made me light-headed.

Nervously, I ran my fingers through my unkempt hair as I rang Bud's bell.

"Bud!" I exclaimed as he opened his door. "Boy, it's good to see you." I opened my arms to embrace him, but he blocked me with his body and shoved me away.

"What do you want?" he said through tight lips.

"Bud," I faltered, "aren't you glad to see me? Just for old time's sake. . . ."

He didn't let me finish. He stepped back and looked at me carefully, then he smiled—a dirty smile.

"For old time's sake? Taken a good look at yourself lately? *What* old times? All I see is a skinny, dirty, haggard old bag, with a big scar on her face."

I winced under his lashing, but I was desperate. I had to have a fix.

"Please, Bud," I begged, "here's ten dollars. Please, please let me have a couple of bags or I'll go right off my head. I may not look like much now, but I *was* your girl once."

"Take your dirty money and get outta here. Yes, you *were* my girl once—a fresh, pretty, clean girl. What you are now doesn't seem possible. Get out, you dirty tramp and don't come back." His words were final; he closed the door.

I didn't dare knock again. I remembered the knife he'd shown me when I left him years before.

I trudged down the stairs and back down the subway steps. All the way up to the Bronx, Bud's words rang in my ears: "A fresh, pretty, clean girl." If only things had worked out differently. If only. . . . I looked at the tracks on my arm. Absently, I picked at the abscess on my sore thumb and stroked the scar on my cheek.

Bud was right, it just didn't seem possible. I had nowhere to go and nothing to look forward to except getting arrested, or maybe murdered—or taking an overdose. Wasn't there a power of some kind that was stronger than drugs? One that could break my chains of addiction and set me free?

CHAPTER • 9

ONE AFTERNOON, late, I was hurrying up the Avenue to my connection, when I heard a voice call my name. I turned and saw only a thin, middle-aged woman coming out of a store.

"Carmen," she repeated. "Don't you remember me? Nancy."

Nancy! It had been a long time since that night she'd showed me the ropes of hustling—since she'd taken me in and shared her room and her works with me. I hadn't seen her in a long time—years, I guess. That's the way it is on the street. One day they're there, the next they're not. You think about them for a while and you ask around; then you're too busy hustling to get high, and when you're high, you don't bother.

I was shocked by her appearance—she looked so old—but I tried not to show it.

"Nancy! Of course I remember you! Where you been! I've missed you."

"Oh, here and there," she said, and smiled. I remembered that smile; it was kind and made you feel sort of good. "How about a cup of coffee?"

I hesitated. I wanted to get off before I went out on the street, but. . . .

"For old time's sake?" as I'd said to Bud.

"Sure," I said, and we turned into a nearby cafeteria.

"How're things with you?" she started off, after we got our coffee and seated ourselves.

"Oh, fine, fine," I lied. "And you? What you been up to?"

"Up to?" Nancy smiled again, faintly. "Upstate, among other things. Oh, I been up to quite a bit, believe me, but I won't bore you. . . ."

I could see she wanted to talk; she *needed* to talk. So I said, "Bore me? Don't be crazy. It's been ages since we've seen each other. Tell me, what all you been up to? It sounds interesting."

"Well . . . ," she hesitated. "There's no good place to start. I got picked up for pros and was sent upstate. I came back to Gene, and you know what *that* was. Finally we broke up. Then I got picked up for drugs, and I made it straight for a while. I even moved back in with my mother, but I got hooked again, and now. . . . Well, now, I got me a little boy. Tommy's two, and he's a doll; I don't know who his father is; I don't care. I got Tommy now. I'm off drugs. I'm taking treatment at the outpatient clinic, and . . . Say, would you . . . ? Oh, no, never mind."

"Never mind what?" I asked. Nancy hadn't been kidding; she'd been up to a lot! She had a kid! I couldn't believe it. The outpatient clinic interested me, too. I wanted to know how she was making out.

"Keep going. Fill me in," I said. "What's the never mind? And how long you been off? What's the outpatient clinic like? Is it any good?" The questions poured out, as hope spurted in me. If Nancy was making it, maybe I could?

"Well," Nancy said, cautiously, "I been off quite a while.

You know how it is . . . you can never be sure. But this time, I really want to. I got Tommy to think of. If I don't look out, Welfare'll take him away from me, and that would really finish me off. I tell you, Carmen, you got no idea what it's like to have a kid!" she said enthusiastically.

"Lotta work, though, aren't they?"

"Oh, yes, but they're a lot of fun, and they look up to you so. I never had anyone look up to me before. Tommy thinks I know everything!"

"I'd like to see him, sometime," I said, not really meaning it. "But tell me about the clinic."

"The clinic? Oh, well, I go there every day. They give me methadone and it tides me over. Before long I hope I'll be off for good. Then Tommy and I are getting out of here. I'm gonna get a job, and. . . ." Her voice trailed off.

"And what?"

"Well, I can't do anything until I finish the treatment, and I can't move from here until I do. It would be just too involved to start with another hospital. Besides, when we go, I don't want people to know Tommy's mother was an addict. Say, would you . . . ?" she said, again.

"That's the second time you've said that. Would I what? Sure I would," I said, without thinking.

"Well, I hate to ask you. . . . Usually Mom sits with Tommy when I go to the hospital, but her sister's sick and she had to go to Brooklyn today. Would you really stay with him while I report in?"

Me baby-sit? The idea floored me. I'd never been near a baby in my life! On top of that, I was itching for a fix.

Nancy noticed my expression. "Oh, forget it," she said. "I knew it was a nutty idea. It's just . . . well, if I don't come, I get in trouble at the hospital."

She got up. "Well, it's been nice seeing you, Carmen. Come by to see us sometime. I'm still at the same old apartment."

"Wait a minute, wait a minute," I said. I couldn't let her go like this, after all she'd done for me. Heck, I ought to be able to baby-sit for a little while; I wasn't a moron.

"What time's your appointment?" I was hoping I could go get my fix and then somehow I'd cope.

"Well, that's one of the troubles—in half an hour. I'll just have to call and see if I can get them to understand. The landlady's got Tommy now, but she's gotta go out herself, so she can't stay."

"I'll do it," I said. "I'll stay with Tommy. I'd like to meet the gentleman."

"Oh, Carmen, thanks a million! I can't tell you how much I appreciate it. He won't be any trouble, I can promise you. Matter of fact, he'll be ready for his nap, so all you'll have to do is sit."

That was a relief! My head was throbbing and my nose was starting to run, but I figured I could stand it another hour, if the kid could. Nancy and I walked quickly to her building, picked up Tommy and went into the familiar apartment.

But it didn't look familiar. Nancy, like Vinnie's uncle, had scrubbed and painted. It was still a small place, but it was cheerful and clean. She had new linoleum on the floor, no more pockmarks to catch your heels, and the sway-backed couch had been replaced by a crib.

Nancy whisked Tommy into the crib expertly, patted his head and headed for the door.

"I won't be long," she said. "Probably only a half hour. At most, an hour. Thanks—thanks again!"

"Oh, save it," I said. Go on."

Tommy and I stared at each other. Then he gave me a tentative smile and said, "Hi."

"Hi," I said back. I felt helpless. What if the kid wanted something? How would I know what to do?

"You better get to sleep," I said pretty fiercely. "Your mama's going to be mad if you don't take your nap right away." I realized I was being pretty ridiculous. You can't scare a kid into a nap. But Tommy lay down obediently, and in a few minutes he was asleep.

I bent over the crib and examined him. He was a cute kid—dark curly hair and a dimple on his cheek. He looked so peaceful; then, all of a sudden, he got up on his hands and knees and starting banging his head against the end of the crib. He was still sound asleep.

"Tommy," I said softly. I didn't want to wake him up. "Cut that out. You'll beat your brains out."

Almost miraculously he stopped hitting his head, but he remained on his hands and knees and rocked his body in a rhythmic way. I was relieved he'd stopped banging his head. I figured at least he wasn't hurting himself, so I walked over the window and let him alone. Maybe, subconsciously, I made him nervous?

As I stood at the window, wiping my nose and getting fidgety, I heard the banging again. There he was, butting his head against the crib again.

I walked back to the crib and spoke to him again. He stopped, but remained in a rocking position. I made several trips back to the crib before Nancy returned, and each time I wondered why the kid acted that way. Did all babies try to beat their brains out? I was getting sicker by the moment, and the banging was beginning to get on my nerves. I wished Nancy would come.

Nancy came hurrying in. "Sorry I was so long. Everything OK?"

"Yeah, I guess so," I answered. But, as I put on my coat, I couldn't resist asking, "Why does he bang his head like that?"

Nancy's face fell. "Did he do it again? I thought he was getting over it," she said.

I was dying for a fix, but I was also dying to know why that kid was so determined to knock his skull in.

"Do all babies do that? Or just Tommy?"

"All drug-addicted babies do," Nancy answered softly. "Or most of them. I was pretty strung out when Tommy was born, and the doctors tell me he was born an addict. Do you wonder why I want to get straight?"

No, I didn't. Teen-ager addicts, maybe, but a baby of two? No, I didn't wonder why Nancy wanted out.

"I can never thank you enough," she started. But I brushed her off. I needed out—for a fix and to think, both.

"Thank you, too," I said and beat it out the door.

I got my fix and went out on the street. I didn't think much until after I got home and was high, and when you're high, your thinking isn't too good. Mine was kinda mushy. I started thinking about my parents. Maybe they weren't so hot, but at least they hadn't started me off like Tommy. I got to be a drug addict by myself; I wasn't born one. Maybe they weren't so bad. Tommy haunted me. He did for quite a while.

Thanksgiving Day came and went. We spent it with Vinnie's mother as we usually did. Usually, we spent Christmas there too. Neither day meant much to Vinnie or his family, but he and I got by, by getting high before we went over.

Somehow the holidays and the thoughts of Tommy made me think of Christmas at home. I knew I could never take Vinnie; he and Dad might kill each other. But I had a yen to see them again—especially Mom—and I remembered the trees we'd had. So maybe we fought, but we had presents and outside decorations and fun at Christmas.

Business had been so slow lately that Vinnie had set up a mugging racket with my tricks. I guess it was my scarred face and the fact that I was pretty strung out. Anyway, business was pretty hard to come by.

One night I saw a young guy talking to some of the girls. I tried to decide whether this man was a cop or not. After watching him for a while, I decided he wasn't, and thought I'd give him a play. I walked by and gave him a smile.

He gave me a big smile back and handed me a booklet. I glanced down at the title and read it aloud, "A Positive Cure for Drug Addiction."

"Are you nuts?" I asked him. "There just isn't any positive cure for drug addiction."

"Ever hear of Teen Challenge?"

"No." I was getting suspicious. Was he a cop?

"I'm John Benton of Teen Challenge," he said, "We have a program that could help you. We have an office in Brooklyn and a girls' home in Garrison, the Walter Hoving Home."

"Do I look like a teen-ager?" I asked.

"Well, hardly," he said. "But, it's difficult to tell. Besides, the average age of our girls is about twenty-five. We started out working with teen gangs and we've just kept the name."

"Have you ever thought about giving your life to Christ?" he continued, "asking Him to change it for you?"

I stared at him; he sounded like Cathy—Cathy of the long ago. Maybe he was on the level. Maybe I better level with him?

"Well, yes. About four years ago I did. A friend got me interested in Christ, but then. . . . Well, then I started on drugs and I haven't thought much more about it. But when Cathy told me about Christ and prayed with me, it helped at the moment. Do you really suppose it still could?"

"Give Christ a chance," the Reverend said. "He really wants to change your life. He can give you the power to change your life."

I wanted to hear more, but I saw Vinnie gesturing to me, to bring the trick down the street so he could mug him. I couldn't let that happen to a minister, I decided, so I told him right off.

"You'll have to excuse me, Reverend, but my friend down the street thinks you're a trick and he's waiting to smack you over the head. I better go tell him who you are."

The minister looked startled, but then his face crinkled into a smile.

"Well, thanks," he said. "Thanks a lot. That's very kind of you. If you ever need us, our address is on the back of that booklet. It's been good talking to you. We'll remember you in our prayers."

Vinnie was furious when I reached him. "Why didn't you bring that guy over here?" he asked.

"He was a minister."

"Oh. Oh." That was all Vinnie said.

We stood there for a few minutes. Vinnie looked up the street, down the street, everywhere but at me. Suddenly he said, "Quick, step back in here."

I drew back into a nearby doorway, then peered out. I couldn't see anyone but an old lady coming along the street.

"When she comes by, I'll grab that handbag dangling by her side," Vinnie explained. "You just beat it. I'll meet you at the apartment, after I cop. Then we can get off."

Vinnie moved in next to me, so that we were both flat against the wall. When the old lady passed by, Vinnie jumped out and reached for the purse. The old lady had a pretty good hold on it. Vinnie jerked hard and the old lady spun around. The purse fell loose and Vinnie grabbed it like a football end going for a touchdown.

The old lady hit the sidewalk with a thud. I started to walk off, afraid she would scream for the cops, but something made me walk back to her side. She was out—out cold. I watched a thin stream of blood trickle from her lips. Her eyes stared blindly upward. I knew I ought to get out fast, but she looked so forlorn, I stayed. It didn't matter much, because a crowd soon gathered around her lifeless body. Someone finally called the police.

Something about that woman got me. I stared down at her. She was anyone's grandmother—gray haired, wrinkled face, a little too plump. I'd never known a grandmother, but. . . . In a way, I could picture Mom looking like that some day.

Under my breath I cursed myself. That money in her

purse was money for my drugs. Would she live? And if she did?

I made my way out of the crowd as a cop pushed his way in. What a way to live! I thought. I might mug my own mother.

Vinnie was there with the stuff when I got back to the apartment. I really needed it. This deal shook me up.

My thoughts kept going back to Mom. It was getting near Christmas, and I guess everyone thinks of home then. I didn't want to go to Vinnie's mother again; it didn't seem like Christmas. I couldn't get Tommy or the old lady out of my mind. I wanted my own mother, desperately—even if she wasn't perfect.

I didn't know about Dad, but I was pretty sure Mom would welcome me for Christmas—or any other time, for that matter. One day, I just picked up the phone and dialed the familiar number.

It rang three times and I was almost ready to give up, when a familiar voice said, "Hello."

"Mom, this is Carmen." I waited, and it seemed like a century before her voice came through again.

"Carmen!" There was another long pause and then Mom's voice came through loud and clear. "Oh, Honey, where have you been? We've been waiting for your call. Where are you? Are you all right?"

"I'm fine, I'm fine," I said, tears trickling down my cheeks. "What about you?"

"Well, right at the moment, your father's in jail. . . ."

"In jail?" I couldn't believe it, and I was beginning to be sorry I'd called. If she was going to start complaining again. . . .

"Actually, it isn't too serious, I think. He ran a stop light and they took him in. He's really been doing real well with his drinking, but what with the holiday parties. . . ." Mom's voice drifted off.

Dad in the jailhouse. That was something for the books! I wanted to laugh, but I knew it wouldn't help Mom any.

"Yeah, I know," I said. "I thought maybe I'd come over for Christmas?"

"Christmas? Oh, fine, fine," Mom said. "I'm not sure when your father will get out, but I'm sure he'll be home by then. You know he always gets the tree and all that stuff."

Dad in the pokey, and Mom as unsure as ever. It sounded like home, all right, but not the merriest of Christmases.

"Well, OK, I'll come out sometime in the afternoon," I said, and hung up.

I spent Christmas Eve hustling. Business was slow and the few tricks I did pick up were drunks on the way home from office parties. When I got back to the apartment, Vinnie was feeling sentimental. He had just opened a bottle of wine, "To celebrate," he said. Wine and heroin don't mix very well, so Vinnie spent most of the night throwing up.

I woke up early Christmas Day. Vinnie was still asleep. I looked around the dreary apartment—no trees, no gifts, no nothing. I dressed quietly and sneaked out.

My spirits lifted on the way to New Jersey. "I'll be home for Christmas," I sang under my breath, as I walked the last few blocks to the house. Love and affection might be missing at our house, but Mom and Dad did have a tree and gifts for each other under it, and a turkey with all the fixings.

When I reached the house, I paused before I opened the door. Maybe I better ring? After all, I was almost a stranger. I rang the bell and Mom answered almost immediately. I threw my arms wide, shouted, "Merry Christmas, Mom," and engulfed her in a bear hug.

She hugged me back, then drew away and gave me a long look. "Come in, come in," she said. "Let's not stand in the doorway all day."

We walked into the living room and I looked at the tree. It was only half-trimmed; Dad was nowhere to be seen. I was disappointed, but I tried not to show it. I put my coat in the hall closet and rejoined Mom who was staring at the tree rather dispiritedly.

I was determined to have a good day, regardless of the tree. "Well," I said gaily, "shall I go ahead and finish the trimming?"

"You can't," Mom said, "until Dad gets back. Most of the bulbs are no good; he went out to see if he could find a store open. He just got out yesterday, so we haven't had much time. Well, I better get back to the kitchen."

I trailed her out there; dinner was just about as far along as the tree. Well, you *are* early, I told myself. "What can I do to help?"

Mom looked at me helplessly and then stared around at the chaos in the kitchen. I was beginning to get irritated, but I choked back a nasty crack and grabbed an apron.

"Shall I fix the stuffing or peel the potatoes?"

"The stuffing, I guess. The turkey'd better get in soon."

Dad walked in just as we got the bird in the oven. Mom had picked up a bit, and things were moving along. I didn't know whether to embrace him or not. I was still scared of him; I'd even brought my knife along, just in case he started anything. I could see the change in him. He looked older, of course, but his manner had changed too—he looked and acted quieter, more subdued.

"Hi, Carmen," he said and patted my shoulder awkwardly. I guess he didn't know what to say or do any more than I did. I got a funny lump in my throat, but I swallowed and said, "Want me to help you finish up the tree?"

"That'd be fine. That'd be fine. I got kind of a late start, you know. I guess your mother told you?"

"Yes, she did. I'm sorry. But two hands and so on," I said, and we pitched in. It looked nice when it was finished. We stood back to admire our handiwork, then Dad went to the closet and pulled out a few packages.

Holy Moses! I'd forgotten to get anything for either of them! What should I do? My determination to be jolly was fast disappearing. I needed a fix, and now this stupidity didn't help matters much. Maybe I could slip out and pick up some things, and maybe, just *maybe* Mom might know a doctor or druggist who would slip me a dolly to tide me over. I decided it was worth a try. I walked out in the kitchen and asked Mom, "How long till dinner?"

"Oh, three hours at least," she said. "Why don't you just sit with Dad until I get through here?"

"Well, I thought I might just run downtown to pick up a few things. You don't know of a doctor nearby who could give me a prescription, do you?"

"A prescription? For what? What's the matter with you?"

"Oh, it's for a sedative," I said lamely. "My nerves aren't too hot lately, "My doctor gives me something called dolophine."

"Dolophine? No, I don't know anybody." She looked at

me peculiarly, as if she were going to say more, then turned away.

Did she guess? I wondered. I was starting to get sick and I knew I'd never last three hours—even one—without a fix of some kind. Then I remembered that Fred had told me about a doctor in Newark who'd sell you a prescription—no questions asked—for fifteen dollars cash on the barrelhead.

"Hey, there's a doctor in Newark I know. That isn't far. Maybe Dad could take me?"

She didn't answer, so I walked into the living room and asked Dad.

"Sure, I'll drive you in. Only take twenty minutes or so."

On the way in, I turned to Dad nervously and asked, "Say, Dad, can I borrow twenty-five dollars? I need it for the doctor; he's kind of expensive. I'm sorry I came off short, but I didn't expect to get sick." I felt kind of guilty asking for an extra ten, but what the heck? He was partly to blame for me being what I was. And maybe with what I had on me, I could pick up a few presents.

"OK," he said shortly, "when we get there. Tell me where to turn."

I directed him to a corner near Dr. Lamb's office, and he parked and fished out a bulging wallet. I didn't feel so bad. He handed me a twenty and a five.

"I'll be back in a few minutes," I said. "There's a drugstore over there, where I can get the prescription filled."

I hopped out and ran into the doctor's office. He saw me in a few minutes and I told him Fred Longman had sent me. The doctor looked at me narrowly and held out his hand. I put the twenty in it and he fished a five out of his desk and handed it back. Then he wrote me the prescription.

I crossed to the drugstore and handed over the prescription. The druggist looked at me briefly, then said, "It'll take a few minutes."

While he was working, I bought a cheap bottle of perfume for Mom and a box of writing paper, and some cigars and a bottle of after shave stuff for Dad. The girl gift wrapped them for me and put them in a plain bag. By that time the prescription was ready, so I paid for all of the things, stuffed the dolophine in the paper bag and went back to the car.

On the way home I popped a dolly into my mouth. I felt lousy; I sure hoped it would work. By the time we reached the house, I was feeling better.

"Thanks, Dad, for helping out," I said, as I laid the presents under the tree. "I feel a lot better now."

I walked out into the kitchen to see if I could help. My eyes almost popped out when I got a look at Mom. She was loaded down with jewelry—four bracelets on each arm, earrings and pins galore, plus several strands of beads. Her purse was on the kitchen table. She jumped when I came into the room and gave me a funny look.

"What gives?" I started, but she interrupted me.

"Dinner's almost ready. Why don't you set the table?"

"OK." If she didn't want to say anything about the junk she had on, all right, I thought. But is she going off her rocker? I set the table and wandered back into the living room. Somehow this day wasn't turning out the way I'd expected. Oh, well, the tree looked nice. Dad had the television on and was drinking a can of beer. I sat down on the couch, nervously. Was he going to get drunk again? He just nodded at me and, as I listened to the Christmas carols, I relaxed and began to sing softly along with the TV performers.

We had a nice dinner; we even talked a little. Over dessert I decided to tell them I was a drug addict. I guess it was being so full, and them trying hard to be nice. Anyway, I just blurted it out.

They both stared at me. "I can't believe it," Dad said.

I rolled up my sleeve and showed them my tracks. He shook his head, and asked: "Carmen, what happened? What went wrong?"

Mom said nothing.

"Well," I replied. "I guess all of us are to blame. The constant fighting that went on here and my own immaturity made me break under the pressure. And one day I found the answer—drugs. I've done almost anything you'd imagine to support my habit: prostituting, mugging, stealing."

Dad started to blame himself. Mom still said nothing. She just eyed me.

Finally she spoke. "I knew it," she said nervously. "I read an article in a magazine not long ago, about a drug addict. She took heroin," she said accusingly. "And she stole all of her mother's jewelry and cash, and a TV set and . . . ." She stopped and her face got beet red, as she saw me looking at her jewelry.

"So! You think I'm nothing but a lousy junkie, come home to rob you!" I screamed at her. "I may be a tramp, a prostitute, a drug addict, but I'd never get low enough to steal from *you.*"

Mom started to cry. She ripped the jewelry off and put it on the table.

"Oh, Carmen, I was so scared when you asked about that dolophine. I didn't know what I was doing." She got up and ran into the living room, grabbing up her purse, in her agitation.

Dad and I sat at the table for a few minutes, then I sighed and got up. I walked into the living room slowly, my mind whirling. Maybe Mom wasn't so wrong. When a person's on junk, nothing matters except getting the money to support one's habit.

I stood in the doorway and looked at my frightened mother, and I realized I *could* do what she feared. It was a pretty crazy scene: there was the tree, still with the unwrapped presents beneath it, and beside it was a woman scared of her own daughter. " 'Tis the season to be jolly!" I thought.

"Oh, Mom," I said and started to cry. I walked over to her and put my arms around her. Slowly, she embraced me and we cried together.

Dad finally appeared in the doorway and looked at both of us. " 'Nother cup of coffee, anyone?" he asked sheepishly.

I sat up and blew my nose and offered Mom my hankie. She smiled shakily and said, "I guess we all could use one."

We sat around, drinking coffee and discussing my problem, for hours. Mom suggested we all move away. "To Colorado or someplace, get out of the metropolitan area, where there aren't any junkies."

"Mom, I could find it if we moved to Timbuctoo," I told her.

Dad suggested a vacation. Deep within me, I was sure there was no way out. That dolly was just temporary relief. I knew I could go to a hospital and get detoxified, but every girl I knew who had done that, had gone right back to the street, as soon as she got out. I listened to their suggestions, and I tried to offer some of my own, but I was pretty halfhearted about it.

Suddenly, Mom said, "I could have you committed! That's what the girl in the magazine story did."

I stared at her. My own mother commit me? How could she do it?

"Carmen, look at yourself," she begged. "You're killing yourself."

I didn't look at myself, I looked at *her*—at my mother. I was killing myself, yes, but I was also killing her, with *my* grief, *my* sorrow, *my* heartache.

"God, oh, God, please help me," she prayed. "Please help Carmen!"

My mother praying! It was the only time I'd ever heard her pray.

"OK, Mom, I'll go," I said quietly.

CHAPTER • 10

I RETURNED TO THE Bronx alone. I dreaded telling Vinnie, but I got a break—he wasn't home. I'd forgotten about it being Christmas; he was at his mother's, of course. I threw a few things in a bag and returned to Jersey.

Next day, Dad went to work and Mom and I talked, and talked, and talked. As a child, I'd never been close to either of my parents—I just couldn't talk to them—but the more Mom and I discussed my problem, the closer I felt to her.

"I'll do whatever I can to help you, after I get you committed," she said earnestly. "I'll visit you, bring you books and stuff. You used to like to read."

I used to like to read, she said. Yes, books had been my first escape from the real world, when I was a kid. First I retreated into a fantasy world of books and then into one of drugs.

"Tell you what, Mom," I said. "I've heard they're much tougher on you if someone else commits you, than if you go voluntarily. Suppose I commit myself? I'll go tomorrow."

"Why, of course. I'll go with you."

I took another dolly before I went to bed. I knew they

gave you methadone in this program I was going to enter, so I was anxious to start it. I knew the dollies wouldn't keep me going forever, and I didn't have too many left.

We left the house bright and early the next morning, and reached the county clerk's office by nine. I was pretty sick, and I didn't read the papers they gave me to sign very thoroughly. The only thing that stuck in my mind was the length of my stay—something about up to thirty-six months.

"How long do I have to stay?" I asked the clerk.

"Oh, three or four months."

I signed the papers and went with two officers from the sheriff's department to the rehabilitation center. Mom waved to me as we drove off.

As soon as I got to the center, I was taken to the dispensary and given a dolly. That helped me get through the signing of more papers and a sort of orientation lecture on the procedures of the center.

I noticed that the windows were painted over on the outside, and all of them were locked. It looked as though the only way they could be opened was with a key.

"How come the windows are painted and locked?" I asked the matron. "To keep us from seeing out? Why?"

"That's not to keep you from looking out. It's to keep outsiders from looking in. We don't want a bunch of curious people staring in like visitors at the zoo. We lock the windows for the same reason: to keep outsiders out, not to keep you in."

I knew she was putting me on, but at least she laughed when she told me that story. She seemed like a good Joe and there was nothing I could do about it, so I smiled back and followed her to the kicking room.

Three of the four beds were occupied. The girls looked up, as the matron introduced me.

"This is Carmen Petra, girls," she said and turned and left me there.

I sat down on the empty bed and the other girls began to bombard me with questions.

"How much stuff do you use?"

"Ten to fifteen bags a day," I said.

"Where do you hang out?"

"The Bronx."

"Hey, I know you," one of the girls cried. "You're Vinnie's old lady, aren't you?"

I wondered what Vinnie was doing. In all the hubbub, I'd forgotten all about him. I bet he was mad as all get out, trying to figure out where I was. Well, this was the last place he'd think of.

The questions kept on coming.

"Who do you cop from?"

"Robert Marshall."

"Hey, man, that guy's got good stuff."

They told me where each of them had hung out, who their connections were and how much stuff they used. The more they talked, the more I wanted out of here. I wanted to be back on the streets, on my way to a fix.

"Say, don't you girls ever talk about anything else?" I asked. "If we're in here to be helped, it doesn't make much sense, does it?

All three girls just stared at me. Then one gave a short laugh and asked, "Something particular you want to discuss?"

I couldn't think of a thing to say, so we all sat in silence for a few minutes.

"Ever been in the gay life?" a girl asked. "We're all gay here."

I was tongue tied. I stared at the three girls, helplessly. I knew that most institutions have their share of Lesbians—hospitals, jails, detention homes, even centers—but it had never occurred to me that I'd get put in a room with three! I spent one whole week in that room, keeping my distance and a careful eye on the girls. They didn't bother me, just ignored me.

At the end of the week, I was moved into a smaller, permanent room, with just one roommate, Daisy. She was a pleasant girl, and we became friends quickly.

She told me she wanted to get out of the center, by the end of the next week, if she could. After my week with the Lesbians, I was pretty anxious to leave, too.

"Can we escape?" I asked.

"Well, I don't really know," Daisy said. "But I can get the window open."

"How?"

Daisy pulled a bobby pin out of her hair and climbed up and stuck it in the lock. Then she put another pin crosswise to the first and used the second one as a handle. I heard a click and she pushed the window open a few inches.

I looked at her admiringly. "Where'd you ever learn to do that?"

"Oh, my old man was a master at this. He taught me." As Daisy pushed the window open a little wider, I clambered up beside her and looked down at the street. It was a long way down; if I jumped I'd never live to brag about my escape.

"What about sheets?" I asked Daisy.

"Nope. We've only got four and that's not long enough.

I've given this a lot of thought; we'd just break our necks if we tried." She gave me a small smile and added, "I guess it's not worth it. Even if you escape, if you get caught, you know, they send you to upstate prison for three years, don't you?"

Three years! Daisy was right; it wasn't worth it. I guessed I could live through three or four months, but three years—never!

The following day I had my first group therapy session with ten girls and a therapist. At first I kept quiet and listened to the other girls, then they started to fire questions at me.

"Why are you ashamed of your father?"

"Why are you a junkie?"

"How many times you been to bed with a guy?"

The answers I gave sounded lame, even to me. I blamed someone else for all my faults—never myself. By the end of that session, I had a lot of things to think about, a lot of questions to ask myself and a lot of true answers to come up with.

After a number of sessions I progressed to the point where I knew who was responsible for my addiction—*me.* I was learning to be honest with myself. A glimmer of hope flickered within me—maybe, just *maybe,* I could be permanently cured.

I asked my counselor how long he thought I'd have to stay, but he evaded the question. When I insisted, he said, "That depends on how you progress."

"Well, I'm making some progress, aren't I? They told me three or four months."

"I don't think you'll make it that soon. It all takes time. There are no shortcuts in this program."

The tone of his voice scared me. "Listen, mister," I said. "I came in here voluntarily and I'll go out the same way, in three, at most four months."

"You didn't read the commitment papers very well, did you? If you're really serious about leaving that soon, you better get yourself a lawyer. The length of your stay here is determined by *us*, not you, as you'd know if you'd read the papers."

I stormed out of the room and back to Daisy. When I poured out the story to her, she looked at me thoughtfully.

"You can write the Legal Aid," she said. "Maybe they can get you out, if you're so set on it."

I went over to the desk and, with Daisy's help, I composed a letter. I wrote that I was being detained under false pretenses. When I was admitted, I had been too ill to understand the commitment papers and had been told by the clerk that I would have to remain only three or four months. That time was almost up, and I wanted out.

About a week later a lawyer showed up. He questioned me on how I'd come in, why I hadn't read the papers and why I wanted to leave.

"Listen, mister, it's just as I wrote you: I came in voluntarily, I was sick and needed help. This place is full of Lesbians and I'm not getting much help. I want out and I want out now!"

The lawyer made some notes, put them in his briefcase and said, "I'll see what I can do for you." Then he walked out and that was the last I ever saw or heard of him.

I wrote more letters—to him and to Mom. She told me the lawyer was doing his best. Finally, I gave up hope and decided to cooperate in the program. I got used to the schedule: up at six; breakfast at seven (the food was as lousy as in all institutions); cleaning chores; group therapy at ten or ten-thirty; lunch at twelve; high-school studies til dinner; dinner at five; TV until lights out, or just rapping with each other.

Finally, the group therapy began to take. It helped me build a new image of myself. At last I could picture myself as never needing drugs again; of living a quiet life in Queens maybe, or Staten Island, in my own apartment; of working as a secretary or a waitress, making good money, living a decent life; maybe even meeting a nice guy and getting married and having four kids.

At the end of seventeen months, they let me out. Saying good-bye to the girls was an emotional binge. Some of them cried, because they weren't leaving, but all of them wished me well and all said the same thing: "Good-bye, Baby, we know you'll make it." Even the girls who'd gone out and were back said the same thing.

I knew I was going to make it. I felt strong. If anyone offered me dope, I'd kill 'em. I had convictions now.

The matron took me to the aftercare clinic and a counselor talked to me for about half an hour. "Report to me every Wednesday," she said, "for a urinalysis. And, young lady, if that test isn't negative, back to the center you come!"

"You can take all the tests you want to," I said. "I'm staying clean; I'm never coming back to this place again!"

She smiled and shook my hand. "See you next Wednesday," she said.

Mom was waiting for me. She kept exclaiming at how well I looked. I'd gained quite a bit of weight, and I was brimming over with enthusiasm about starting a new life.

We took the train home. Dad wasn't in from work yet. I hadn't seen him since I left home. Mom had told me he'd been working hard; his accident had cost him quite a bit, and he was trying to make it up. When he finally came in, he just grunted, "Glad to see you." I wasn't sure whether I was a bother or a blessing.

The next day I went over to CADA (Citizens Against Drug Abuse). The counselor at the center had told me there was a branch in our neighborhood, run by two former drug addicts. She also told me that CADA had helped a lot of girls keep straight. They held group therapy sessions for ex-addicts and addicts who were trying to quit.

Everyone there seemed glad to see me, and I was eager to tell my story, if it would help someone get straight. I practically lived at CADA for a while and I felt I was encouraging and helping some who were wavering. I knew if I went back to the Bronx or saw Vinnie, I'd probably wind up hooked again, so I told them to stay away from their old haunts and their old friends. I told them Vinnie was out of my life forever. I didn't write to him. I didn't think about him.

I met a couple of girls at CADA who were real friendly. One night Lil invited me over to her place. She lived in a real nice house and I admired the furniture and draperies. She took me down to the recreation room in the basement. It was lovely. I stared around admiringly. Then the jolt came.

"Want me to turn you on, Carmen?" Lil asked.

I stared at her unbelievingly as she offered me some hashish. I sputtered that I wasn't interested and that she shouldn't have any either, but she ignored me and lighted up. As I smelled the hashish and watched Lil's eyes get dreamy, the old craving came over me. The next thing I knew, I was high.

When I came off it, the world had crumbled. Here I'd spent seventeen months in hell to get over my addiction —now those seventeen months were just so many ashes. I hated myself. Would it be long before I'd be using a needle again?

That happened on Saturday. The following Wednesday I went to the aftercare clinic. Mrs. Parker, the counselor, said the tests were negative and to come back the next week.

When I got home, I decided I'd better find something to do besides hang out at CADA. I spent the rest of the day studying the want ads. Next day, I made the rounds looking for a secretarial job. My typing wasn't good enough, I was told, and I returned home discouraged.

Mom gave me a pep talk that night and I set out again the next day and finally landed a job as a waitress. It was a crumby, dirty joint, and I was a pretty lousy waitress, so after four days I left. It was a sort of mutual agreement: the owner didn't actually fire me, and I didn't actually quit.

Lil called the next weekend. I was bored, so I went over to her house again. We couldn't smoke hashish because her parents were home and she didn't want them to smell it. But she had some pills—Cebas, she said. I took one and was off again.

This time, when I got home, my conscience bothered me even more than it had the week before. Also, I was scared about going to the center on Wednesday. Suppose the test turned out positive? I worried all weekend. Finally, I decided I'd go to CADA and make a clean breast of the whole thing to Ned, the leader, on Monday.

Ned heard me out in silence. Then he looked at me scornfully. "Sorry! I'm sorry!" he mimicked in a falsetto voice. "Don't give me that. I just don't buy it. One day, you're in here holier than thou telling the kids how clean you are—the next you're lapping up hashish and God knows what else. Your example could send those kids to an early grave. Don't tell *me* you're sorry!"

"But I really am," I protested. "I don't know what made me give in. I'll do anything you tell me to make up for it. Anything—honest."

"All right, we'll see how sorry you are." Ned pulled a pair of scissors out of his desk, grabbed me by the hair and started hacking at it. It was very long—I hadn't had it cut since I'd gone to the center—and Ned knew it was my pride and joy.

But this was my punishment. I sat there silently. A few tears trickled down my cheeks, as he cut and cut and cut. Ned put the scissors down on the desk and I stared at the pile of hair on the floor.

"All right," Ned said. "Every time you look in the mirror, remember why your hair was cut. Look in that mirror and say—and *mean*—'I'm never going to touch drugs again.' Now, get in that lavatory and scrub it clean. There's a rag under the sink."

I had heard of this kind of punishment before. The combination of the haircutting and the lavatory was supposed to be a reminder I'd never forget. I got up, walked into the lavatory and bent and picked up the rag. I didn't want to look in the mirror. I forced myself to wet the rag and start cleaning the floor, but the mirror drew me like a magnet.

I stared at my reflection. Ned had left me little more than a fringe. I stared at my tearstained face and vowed that I would never, *never* smoke pot or hashish, pop pills or shoot heroin again.

By the time I finished cleaning the lavatory, I was feeling

a little sorry for myself and not quite so repentant. Surely Ned would say something to bolster my confidence.

He didn't; he just looked at my shorn head and turned back to his desk.

When I got home I started worrying again about what Mrs. Parker, the counselor, would say or do on Wednesday. Ned wasn't much help there, that was for sure. Having short hair and cleaning a john certainly wasn't going to change my urinalysis, and it was obvious Ned wasn't going to put in a good word for me.

By evening, I was still sore at Ned and still scared about going to the center. What was the use? I asked myself. I'll never make it, and I'm sure not going back to that hell hole again. I picked up the phone and called Lil.

"Hey, come on over," she said. "Gotta couple of dates here."

I went on over and met the boys. One was a junkie and as soon as he saw me, he knew a kindred soul. "Why don't we go over to Brooklyn?" he asked.

We all piled into a car and took off. The junkie soon found a connection and he returned to the car with four bags of heroin. Neither Lil nor her date had ever shot heroin before so I tried to get them to snort it, instead of mainlining, but they both insisted they wanted to do it "like you." So I drilled them both, and, of course, they both got sick. I laughed; it reminded me of my first time.

That shot sucked me right back into my old life. I knew I couldn't go back home; I didn't want to go back home. As I sat in the car, nodding, I thought of Vinnie and the Bronx. Well, why not?

CHAPTER • 11

I WANDERED DOWN Westchester Avenue, and saw nothing but new faces. It had been over two years since I'd left, but I'd no idea everyone would be gone. Then I recognized Barry. I'd never been too crazy about him, but it sure was good to see a familiar face.

"Barry," I said. "What's new?"

Barry stared at me for a minute, then he started to laugh. "Well, Carmen! Where in the world you been? I haven't seen you around in ages. Boy, you certainly look good," he said admiringly.

"I've been in a drug program," I replied shortly.

"What you doing here, then? If you're planning on staying clean, you better get out of here."

"I know, I know. But I wanted to see Vinnie."

"Vinnie? You mean you haven't heard?"

I knew from the tone of Barry's voice that something dreadful had happened. He couldn't be dead, could he? But he was.

"Vinnie died about a year ago—an OD," Barry told me. Someone found him on a rooftop, dead."

Vinnie is dead; Vinnie is dead. The words rang in my mind, but I couldn't believe them. I hadn't wanted him around, but I didn't want him dead, either; I just didn't want him around. It was a crazy situation; I was half-glad, half-sorry. Vinnie was gone out of my life forever; I couldn't blame him anymore.

"Carmen, I'm sorry," Barry's voice interrupted my whirling thoughts. "I never guessed you didn't know, you being his old lady, and all. I'm sure sorry," he repeated and he started to back away. "I gotta be goin'. See you around . . . I mean . . . I hope . . . I *don't* see you around."

He turned and fled. I was alone on the corner of Westchester and Simpson. How many years had it been since I'd first stood there alone? Too many. Vinnie was gone, my parents were gone, Ned was gone, even Mrs. Parker was gone. No one could help me now.

It wasn't long before I picked up a trick and then another and another. I stayed high all that night. From now on, all the money I made could be spent on me alone. No more Vinnie to get off first; no more Vinnie to support. I could take care of myself, now.

For six straight months, I lived it up—stayed on an almost perpetual high—and I started drinking, too. Booze and drugs don't mix too well for most junkies. but I didn't have too much trouble mixing them. I earned myself a mean reputation for being fast with a razor and a knife. The street respected me and let me alone—no one messed with Carmen.

One night I got pretty drunk. Two women sitting down the bar from me were staring at me and whispering. I didn't like it; I didn't like it one little bit, I decided.

"Something you don't like about my face?" I asked. Neither answered, so I staggered over to them and repeated my question. When they still refused to answer,

I grabbed one of the women and shook her.

"Get your hands off her," the other commanded.

That did it. I exploded with anger. I reached over and slapped the woman square in the face. "No one gets smart with Carmen," I said, "not and gets away with it." I reached up to slap her again, but both women were on their feet now, swarming all over me.

Their long nails raked my face, and one yanked me by the hair, until she held handfuls of it. I flailed out as best I could, but I was too drunk to be a match for them. I fell to the floor and the last thing I remember was a bar stool coming at my face.

I came to in the emergency room of the hospital. The doctor had just finished stitching up my forehead. My head ached from the wound and all the booze, but I tried to answer the inevitable questions of the cops. I couldn't tell them much, so they finally let me go.

I made it back to the bar, determined to kill the women, but they'd left long since. I had a drink to settle my head and then went back to my room and slept until noon.

Back on the street, who should I bump into but Fred, the guy who knew Doc Lamb in Newark. Fred'd been a pusher in the old days; I was sure glad to see him. We went through all the business about being glad to see you, then Fred said, "Carmen, I got news for you."

"Yeah, man," I said. "Something sweet? Like you're giving away free dope?"

"Nope," he replied cheerfully. "I'm off the stuff. That's my news."

I laughed. "Well, goodies for you. Those are familiar words. Seems to me I've said that, too. When'd you get out? Yesterday?"

"No, I'm serious. I've been straight for over two years."

"You had to do two years? Boy, that's a long time! Where'd they send you, upstate?"

"Teen Challenge."

"Teen Challenge? What's that?" I asked. "Oh, wait a minute, I do remember hearing about it. Don't tell me it really works?"

"Well, what really works is Christ. He's the One who changed my life," Fred said, simply.

I was still skeptical. I'd been through too many *cures*. But. . . . "Tell me about it," I told Fred.

Here's the story he told me:

Two summers ago, a minister named Arthur James came on the block. He told addicts about a cure and he gave Fred a tract called "A Positive Cure for Drug Addiction." Fred read it and decided he had nothing to lose. He went to Teen Challenge and two weeks later was admitted to the program.

He lived at the Boys' Home in Brooklyn for two months, then went to a farm in Rehrersburg, Pennsylvania, for nine more. Now, he had a job and was living in the re-entry home of Teen Challenge.

"And the wonderful part is that Christ wants to change your life, too, Carmen," Fred finished.

"I'm glad for you, Fred. Honest, I am, but it won't work for me. I've tried everything—jail, hospital, a rehabilitation program—nothing will ever work for me."

"That's exactly the shape I was in," Fred said. "I'd even been to Kentucky. But I'd never let Christ into my life—not really. It was all so easy. When I *really* asked Him to come in, and when I sincerely wanted to live for Him, He changed my life. If I didn't believe that, Carmen, I wouldn't be here."

I couldn't get over how well Fred looked—how healthy—and he had a certain peace about him. "You actually think there's hope for me?" I asked, half-wanting to believe, but afraid to take a chance again.

"I *know* there is. Come to the Girls' Home," he urged. "You'll see girls there who have been clean for years."

Fred seemed so positive, so sure. I wished I could be, but, deep in my bones, I felt the only real change I could ever experience was death. Yet I was afraid to die.

"Come on to the Center with me, *now,*" Fred pleaded. "Talk to Brother Benton, the Director of the Home."

"Do they give you medication?" I asked cautiously.

"No."

"Sorry, Fred. I know I could never kick cold turkey." I wanted to say "Yes, " but it just didn't seem worth it. Teen Challenge was, after all, just another program.

Fred made one more play. "Remember how strung out I used to get? Always scheming, always angling? Well, Christ changed all that, and if He can change me, Carmen, He can change you. He helped me when I was kicking bad, and so did the staff members. Believe me, there's always someone there who will pray with you. They stay up with you, when you're kicking. Best of all, God will help you. You can make it, Carmen.

"I'm happy for you, Fred. I am, I am; but it's not for me," I said, and walked away.

Fred came back again about a week later and tried again. His words had stayed in my mind, but I was still afraid to try another program. I refused again.

That night I really hung one on. At closing time, Andy the bartender wanted to take me home, but I insisted I could make it alone. I staggered out into the raw, blustery night and made it to my connection.

"Carmen, you better be careful," she said, as she held out two bags. "You're pretty drunk. You better save both of these for morning. Why don't you just go home and hit the sack?"

I gave her what I hoped was an icy stare, grabbed the bags and headed back to my room. As I tried to get the key in the lock, Chester, my next-door neighbor opened his door. Chester was a little old man, who drank quite a bit now and then, but he never touched drugs. Occasionally he came to my room and he always paid promptly.

"Hi, Chester," I said. And then I decided I'd get off, before I went in. Chester watched me weave down the hall to the bathroom we shared.

"Take it easy, Carmen," Chester said. "Why don't you come in and have a cigarette with me, before you hit the sack?"

"Cigarette? That sounds like a good idea. But you bring one to me," I said groggily. "I don't wanna go to your room."

He put his hand on my arm, as though to draw me to his room, but I shrugged loose.

"Oh, come on, Chester, get lil ole Carmen a cigarette, like a good boy," I coaxed.

He shrugged, went into his room, came back with a cigarette and lighted it for me.

"That's a good boy, Chester. Don't you worry. Carmen can take care of herself," I said and walked into the bathroom and locked the door.

I cooked up and stuck the needle in my arm. That's the last thing I remember clearly. Suddenly, I felt as though I were on fire. I was burning up, but I could see no flames.

I got up, slowly, painfully. I leaned against the washbasin and looked into the small mirror. A hideous, swollen face stared back at me out of puffed-up eyes. The face seemed to have no lips, just a gaping hole, and no hair. The ears were bent and twisted out of shape.

I put my hands up to my own face—they were as burned and blistered as that staring face. Only then did I realize that stranger was me. Only then did I realize what had happened to me—I had overdosed!

I began to scream. "Help me, help me!" I heard footsteps in the hall and a body crashed against the door. Then Chester's voice called, "Carmen, open up! Open up! The door's locked."

Pieces of burned skin peeled off my fingers as I struggled with the door. I thought my fingers would come out of their sockets. Finally the lock gave way and Chester fell in.

"What have you done to yourself? My God, what have you done?" he cried.

I couldn't answer him; I didn't *know* what I'd done. I stared into the mirror again, and smelled the acrid odor of singed hair and charred material.

"I guess my hair caught fire from the cigarette," I said weakly, "and my blouse from that?"

"I've got to get you to the hospital before you die," Chester said, and took hold of me gingerly.

"No, no! I can't stand the pain of kicking now. Please don't call an ambulance. Just give me a drink; that'll help more than anything right now."

Chester helped me to his room, got me a drink and

watched me gulp it down. Then, again, he started insisting I go to the hospital.

I sat there all night, trying to figure out what to do. No one would want me in this condition. How could I support my habit? I watched my hands swell beyond all recognition. I didn't dare look in a mirror; I was too afraid.

Finally, the pain got so bad I agreed to go with Chester. He took me to the hospital in a cab, and they gave me a medication immediately. I slept while the doctors worked over me, and woke, drowsily, to find myself swathed in bandages. I lifted my bandaged hands awkwardly, trying to discover what my face was like, but all I could feel were three small holes: one for my mouth, one for my nose and one for my left eye.

I tried to reconstruct what had happened, but I was too groggy. I dozed, woke and dozed again for almost a week.

In the two months I spent in that hospital, I pieced the nightmare together after a fashion. When I overdosed, I must have fallen to the floor and the cigarette set my hair afire. I guess I must have tried to beat it out with my hands.

That two months was the worst I ever spent in my whole life. I got an ear infection and they had to feed me intravenously; the pain from the burns was nearly intolerable, even though they kept me under sedation. Worst of all was the agony of withdrawal, from both alcohol and drugs.

When they released me, they gave me some pain pills and I stayed high on those for two days. The third day I managed to get some heroin.

I bought a long wig and went back on the street. By artful draping, I covered my misshapen ears and the scars on my cheeks, which healed quite well. I didn't have too hard a time. Some of my old customers had heard of my accident and they were sympathetic.

Shortly after I got out, I ran into Fred again. He knew about my accident, and was very sympathetic. He told me he was going to Bible School now and some day would be a minister. Again he begged me to go to Teen Challenge. Again I refused.

That summer I got busted again—fifteen days for pros. As soon as I got out, I went right back to the needle.

Winters are the worst, and this winter was one of the coldest I could remember. I hated winter. When you start to feel sick, you feel cold enough; you don't need the weather to make it worse. Only a real high makes you warm.

One bitterly cold night I bumped into Irene, a friend from years back. She gave me the same message as Fred: "Go to Teen Challenge. Christ changed my life and He can change yours, too."

"You too?" I couldn't believe it. Irene had been on drugs for over fourteen years.

"Yep, me too," she said. "I'm married now and we live out in Pennsylvania near the Teen Challenge Training Center at Rehrersburg."

It was Irene who finally sold me on the program. If, after fourteen years, Christ had changed her life, I decided I'd give Him a chance at mine. I agreed to go see the director of the Girls' Home the next day.

WHAT KIND OF people are in this building? I wondered, as I stared at the two-story blue and white building at 444 Clinton Avenue. Now that I was here, I was afraid to go in.

"They're human beings, that's for sure, Carmen," I scolded myself. "Go on in."

I took a deep breath, pulled open the gate and marched up to the glass door.

"Your name please?" a pleasant-looking receptionist asked.

"I came to have an interview with the Reverend Benton."

She motioned me to a chair and picked up her phone. "This is Nan. Carmen Petra is here and she wants an interview."

The girl nodded several times, hung up and told me, "Go through that door at the end of the hall and on up to the second floor, and the receptionist will take you to Brother Benton's office."

I followed her directions, and just as I started up the stairway I was nearly knocked over by someone hurrying behind me. I turned around, indignantly, and my jaw dropped open. It was Vinnie! But it couldn't be Vinnie—Vinnie was dead. I fumbled at the door and tried to get out.

"Carmen!" Vinnie shouted. "Carmen! Oh, it's good to see you. Well, aren't you going to say anything?"

"But, Vinnie," I mumbled, "it can't be you. You . . . you're dead! Or are you?" I was shaking, I was so scared.

"Well, yes and no," Vinnie laughed.

He sounded like Vinnie; he acted like Vinnie—always talking in riddles. But I was in no mood for games; I was too shook up.

"Look," I snapped, "this is no time to be funny. Somebody told me you died of an overdose. What happened?"

"Yeah, I heard that rumor, too, when I was up at the Teen Challenge Farm in Pennsylvania. But you oughta know how it is. You were on the street long enough. Someone gets busted, does a couple of years and the rumors start flying. He isn't seen on the block and the next thing you know he's gone OD.

"The old Vinnie *is* dead," he continued. "But the new one is very much alive and rarin' to go."

He looked rarin' to go, too. His face was tanned and he'd put on weight. We sat on the bottom step and he told me what had happened. His story was a lot like Fred's: he'd been hanging out on the block and he'd wandered down to listen to some people singing on the next corner. It turned out to be a Teen Challenge street meeting. A group was singing gospel songs. Then former addicts testified on how Christ had changed their lives. Like Fred, he was impressed, and, like Fred, he was back at the center in Brooklyn, working as a junior staff member.

"Next month I'm going up to the Teen Challenge Bible School in Rhinebeck," Vinnie wound up. Then he took my hand. "Carmen, Jesus wants to change your life, too," he said.

There was such a radiance about Vinnie when he spoke about Christ!

I lowered my head and tears rolled down my cheeks. "I know, Vinnie," I said. "That's why I'm here. Do you really think there is any hope for me? There isn't time to tell you everything, but I'm about at the end of my rope."

"Sure, there's hope. And there's time to fill me in quickly, too. Go ahead, what you been doing?"

I pulled myself together and managed to give him a brief rundown on my seventeen months at the center, about CADA, about the fire. . . . When I mentioned the fire Vinnie took a long look at my face. I braced myself for his reaction.

"You're just the type Christ wants," he said and he traced the scar on my forehead gently with his fingertip. "Your desperate need will help you. You're going to make it, Carmen, I know it."

"Good lord," I said. "I'm supposed to be upstairs being interviewed. I better beat it."

"I'll see you around. I live here—will for another month before I go to Bible School. Tell Brother Benton you know me," Vinnie said, and he gave me a little push up the stairs and walked on out of the door.

Vinnie's enthusiasm was infectious. My spirits mounted as I climbed the stairs. Maybe there was hope? I remembered Vinnie's voice saying, "Let's get off—me first." Now he talked of Christ. His voice used to be filled with hate; now it radiated love.

The receptionist directed me down the hall to the office of the Director of the Girls' Home. When I opened the door,

I saw the same man I'd met years ago up in the Bronx.

"Hello there, I'm Reverend Benton," he said, and motioned me to a seat.

"Why did you come here?" he asked.

"I'm a drug addict, and I know a fellow by the name of Vinnie," I blurted. What a beginning!

"Oh yes, Vinnie. He's a great guy. God's really done a great job in his life. Now, how long have you been an addict?"

"About six years."

"Do you really want to get rid of your habit? Do you really want to get straight?"

"Yes," I said fervently. "Yes, yes! I do."

"How'd you hear about Teen Challenge?"

"Well, *you* told me about it a long time ago, but I didn't pay much attention," I said sheepishly. "But not long ago Fred and Irene, old friends of mine, sold me on your program."

The minister laughed when I mentioned that he'd told me about it. Then he sobered and said, "Carmen, our program is Christ-centered. You have to understand that, right off. We believe that Christ can give you the power to overcome your habit. We are *not* a bunch of religious nuts, but we do believe—strongly—that Jesus wants to change your life."

As he talked on about Christ and about the program, my mind wandered a little. I wondered how strict they were. I'd heard religious places were pretty tough; I wondered if there were any Lesbians here. Most of all, I wondered if the program would really work for me.

The reverend was still talking. I concentrated on listening.

"The whole program is voluntary. We ask you to stay a year, but if you don't want to, you don't have to. If you don't *really* want to be in the Girls' Home, we don't want you there. We try to create a home atmosphere there, rather than that of an institution. My wife and I and our three children live there, along with the staff and our girls."

"What happens at the end of the year?"

"We encourage our girls to go on to Bible School. Most of them do, but under certain circumstances some don't. Have you any children, by the way?"

"No."

"Ever been married?"

"No." Vinnie flashed through my mind, but we'd never been married.

"Have you ever been in jail?"

"Yes."

"How many times?"

"Four."

"Having been with groups of girls before, then, you know that our Home is not heaven. We have some girls who are just not for real—real phonies. We are patient with them, when they first come in, but if they don't straighten up and seek Christ, we ask them to leave. You can't make it in our program, on someone else's coattails. If you're going to make it, you make it with just Christ and yourself. You'll see a lot of girls who do make it, though, and that should encourage you."

He paused for breath and then continued solemnly, "We are serious about what we are doing. To me, it is a matter of life or death for our girls. Some, we will never be able to help. They came from the streets and they stayed such a short time. I can't help them any more, they are dead."

I thought of some of the girls I knew. Yes, many were dead.

"I know what you mean," I said.

He pulled a folder from his desk and handed it to me. "I want you to read this material carefully, Carmen. It gives you our schedule, our rules and what we expect of you, as well as an explanation of the spiritual side of our program. Take your time and read it all over. I'll be back in a little while and will answer any questions you may have." He nodded and walked out of the office.

I opened the folder and started to read the welcoming message from the staff. He didn't have to warn me to read this stuff carefully; after my seventeen months at the center, I was going to read it word by word. Never again was I going to sign anything I didn't understand every word of.

There didn't seem anything in it I couldn't go along with. The no-smoking rule and kicking cold turkey would be rough, but if I had help, maybe I could make it. The religious aspect didn't bother me; it sounded a lot like my old friend Cathy, rather warm and nice.

The door opened and Brother Benton walked in. He smiled at me, and asked, "Well, any questions about the Walter Hoving Home procedures? What do you think? Still want to come in?"

"Sure do. When can I come?"

"Remember, Carmen, if you enter our program, you will have to sign a statement saying that you have read this folder and that you understand this is a Christ-centered program. If you are to continue in our program you will be expected to give your life to Christ."

"I understand. What and where do I sign?" I answered, and repeated, "When can I come?"

"How about today?"

"Today?" I was a little flustered. I didn't have any clothes or anything.

"There's one empty bed left up in Garrison. You can have it. I just saw Vinnie and he said to tell you he was praying for you. By the way, he went looking for you, a couple of times, when he got a pass from the farm, but he couldn't locate you. Right now, he's in the chapel, praying and thanking God you're here."

"Vinnie praying for me?"

The reverend grinned. "Sure. We do a lot of that around here. We're always praying for each other. We're all in the soup together, and all of us need help."

I was impressed. I guess they really do care about a person here.

"But I don't have any clothes, or even a toothbrush," I stammered.

"Oh, don't worry about that. We have friends who donate a lot of clothes. You're pretty frail looking, but I think we can scare something up that will fit. If not, we'll just take it in a little. My wife, and several of the staff, are pretty good at sewing."

"OK. Let's go," I said, and grinned back.

We had supper at the center and then the Reverend Benton and I took off for Garrison. It took us about an hour from Brooklyn, and I was half asleep when we drove up the long driveway. It had really been a busy day.

Mr. Benton pointed out the swimming pool as we drove through the stately old trees that lined the driveway. I could see acres and acres of green, green grass stretching out beyond.

"We have a horse, too," he told me, as we pulled up in front of a beautiful three-story, English-style mansion.

This is a Girls' Home, I thought. Boy, it looks like a summer resort! I woke up with a bang, and my spirits soared. What a wonderful place to live.

He pulled around in the back and parked. As we rounded the corner on our way to the front door, he beckoned to a girl standing nearby.

"Wanda, this is Carmen. She's just starting our program," he said.

"Hi. We're glad you've come," Wanda said. She walked with us up to the big oak door and as he opened it, she knelt and took her shoes off. I looked at her in amazement. Boy, this really was a religious place! But I bent over and started to remove my shoes, too.

The Reverend Benton laughed. "No, no, you don't have to take your shoes off. Unless you like to go barefoot, like Wanda?"

He was still laughing as he led me into the hall, onto thick green carpeting. I gaped at the beautiful furniture and draperies, not noticing a woman who came toward us.

I felt an arm around my shoulder and a gentle voice say, "Welcome home, Carmen. We're glad to have you. I'm sure you're going to like it here. At least, we hope so."

"This is my wife, Elsie, Carmen," the reverend said. "Elsie, this is Carmen Petra."

Mrs. Benton introduced me to some of the staff and to a few girls. Everyone greeted me warmly. This place certainly was different from any other place I'd been. It must be the feeling of concern and love, I decided.

Eileen Arnold, the Assistant Director of the home, led

me into the office. She pulled out a folder like the one I'd read in Brooklyn.

"Did you read this?" she asked, in a very friendly way.

"Yes."

"If you've no questions, and you understand it fully, then just sign this paper and it will become a part of your permanent record."

I signed and then she asked me a lot of questions—personal questions about myself and how I felt about things, not just name, address, parents, age, like at the other places.

Then she handed me an application form to fill in, and she helped me fill out the medical history form.

She sat back in her chair a moment and then started to talk. "Once a month you'll have a chance to sit down with one of the staff and go over your progress for that period. You'll have monthly tests in your classes, but you don't have to worry too much about either the tests or the get-togethers. We're here to help you, not hurt you. We hold the progress get-togethers so we can help you. If you have any weak points, we want to help you strengthen them. Remember, we're here to *help* you," she repeated.

"What's your religious background?"

I was embarrassed; I really didn't have any. Weakly, I dredged up Cathy, and that was it. I apologized that I'd had no more.

"Oh, don't feel bad. We're concerned with what you are now—not with your past. Most of all, we're concerned with what you're going to be! Jesus will cleanse you of sin, so your past will be forgiven. That is the wonderful part of the gospel."

It sounded good, especially that part about my sins. For

sure, I wanted them forgiven. They were many. Just before I left her office, Eileen prayed for me. She asked Jesus to make himself real to me. I joined her and begged Him to come into my heart. I really needed Him.

Eileen took me to the kicking room, on the main floor, just off the living room. I slept like a log that night, but by the time morning came, I was starting to feel sick. As the day wore on, it got worse. If only I had a cigarette, I thought, that would help some. I know I've got to kick the drugs, but a cigarette . . . ?

Finally, I got up and walked up to the next floor. I figured maybe I could find a butt someplace. I was so fidgety, I couldn't stay still. When I opened the door to the next floor, I bumped into Barb, a girl I'd met the night before. She'd only been here a week or two.

"Say, Barb, know anyplace I can get a cigarette? This kicking cold turkey is rough. If I could just have a drag or two, it might help."

"Yeah, kicking's no fun. I know. Tell you what—I've got a few cigarettes left. You go get dressed. Dig up one of the staff and tell 'em you're so fidgety, you're going out for some air. I'll meet you down on the small bridge by the pool."

I ran downstairs, threw my clothes on and reported, as Barb had directed, that I was going out. No one seemed to object. Barb was waiting on the bridge. She reached into her bra, drew out two cigarettes, handed me one and lighted it, and then her own.

I drew the smoke down deeply into my lungs. It tasted wonderful and I smoked it down until it burned my fingers.

"How about another?" I asked hopefully.

"Nothing doing. I've only got three left. Meet me tomorrow and I'll let you have another. Then it'll be up to you."

"How'd you get them?" I asked her, on the way back to the house.

"Nothing to it. The staff took a bunch of us into town last week. Another girl kept an eye out for me and I ran into the drugstore and bought a pack and stuffed it in my bra. It was kinda' bulky, but then so am I, so nobody noticed."

Well, I guessed I didn't need to worry about the no smoking rule too much, if it was that easy to break.

I went back to the kicking room, undressed and got back into bed. The cigarette had helped some, but my nerves were raw. I needed a fix and I knew it was going to be worse. I tossed; I turned. I thought about leaving, but where would I go? I had no money, nothing.

One of the staff stuck a head in the door and asked what I wanted for supper. Supper? The mere thought of food made my stomach turn over. I shook my head, and the door closed.

As the night wore on, I got worse. My stomach heaved like a boat in a wild ocean. Every time I turned over, it churned wildly. From time to time, the door opened and a staff member asked, "How are you doing?"

It was a pretty stupid question. They could see I was a wreck. I decided I didn't want someone hanging over me, praying over me. I felt bad enough. Each time, I managed to croak out, "OK."

Sometime, I don't know what time, my stomach really went overboard. I started a long series of trips to the bathroom. Vaguely, I was glad I'd turned down supper—at least that wasn't there to lose. I heaved until my muscles were sore, and it didn't seem possible I could get sick again.

I crept back into bed one more time, praying and hoping this would be the last time. The door opened and I heard the familiar, "How are you doing, Carmen?"

I was too weak to even answer. This time, the questioner leaned over my bed. I turned over gingerly; I didn't want my stomach to start quaking again, and looked up.

"I'm Janet Downes," the girl said, "one of the staff. I heard you weren't doing too well, so I'll just stay up here with you for the rest of the night."

"You don't need to. . . ." I started and then my stomach heaved again. I didn't even have time to get out of bed. When I stopped retching, I found my voice.

"I'm sorry," I whispered. "I'll. . . ."

"Forget it," Janet said. "I'll clean up. That's what I came for—to help."

She went into the bathroom and came back with some towels. I turned away while she finished cleaning up. I was afraid to watch.

"Thanks," I muttered. "Janet, I'm not sure I'm going to make it. I'm so sick, so weak. I feel as though I were in a trap—a pit—and can't get out."

"Do you want me to pray for you?"

I felt so lousy I was willing to try anything. "Please do," I managed. "Just pray that I make it through the night."

She put her hand on my shoulder and asked Jesus to heal me and to take away the sickness. It was a short prayer, but sincere.

My stomach was quieting down a little, so I asked her, "Janet, do you really think I can make it?"

"Sure you will—if you put your trust in Christ. The girls

who make it are those who let Christ be Lord and Saviour of their lives. You can do that, can't you?"

"I guess so," I said, meekly. It sounded simple. But I'd been too busy with my stomach to ask the Lord or anyone else to help me. I was too sick.

As I struggled through the rest of the night, Janet told me a little about herself. She was a Bible School graduate of Bethany Fellowship, and a graduate nurse as well. I figured she was a pretty good nurse; she sure had a lot of compassion.

"How long you going to sit up with me?" I asked. I could see the sky lightening in the windows behind her.

"Just a little longer. Sally Smythe will be here before long. She'll stay as long as you want her. We try to take shifts when a girl kicks hard."

I fell asleep, at long last. When I awoke, the sun was high in the sky.

I turned over cautiously; I shook my head. Everything was quiet.

"I'm *really* feeling better," I said aloud. "Maybe the Lord *is* on my side."

I got up, pulled my clothes on and walked into the living room. Two girls were cleaning and dusting.

"What time is it?" I asked.

"Three-thirty," one girl replied, after glancing at the clock on the mantel.

"Boy, I really did sleep!" I was a little embarrassed; here were these girls working away and I'd just gotten up.

"Good," said the girl who'd told me the time. "You must be starved. Why don't you go out to the kitchen: Mom Downes is probably fixing supper now."

I walked through the dining room into the kitchen. A

woman, dressed in white, was standing at the stove cooking meat. I hesitated. After all, it was the middle of the afternoon, and she was cooking supper. How could I ask for breakfast?

Mrs. Downes turned around. "Hungry?" she asked.

"Well, yes."

"Come on in and sit down. Just let me turn this stove down and I'll rustle something up. What do you want—orange juice, apple or tomato?"

"Orange, please."

She reached into the big refrigerator, pulled out a half-gallon of juice and poured me a big glass. It tasted wonderful.

"What about soup? Noodle? Split pea? Vegetable beef? Only take a minute."

"Noodle sounds fine," I said. "Boy, this place is like a restaurant—meals any hour of the day."

"Just for the new ones," she said, as she put the soup in front of me. "We know they need it. Not that you can't get a snack in between—but after you settle in, you've got to settle on whatever I cook!" She laughed and returned to the stove.

"Well, from the smell of it, that won't be too hard," I said, and started in on the soup and crackers she'd put alongside. As I ate, I marveled at why she was so nice to me. What was she getting out of it? Why was everybody so good to me? Why did they really want me?

I went back to the kicking room and lay down, fully clothed, and had a nap. It was about five when I awoke and I really felt wonderful. I thought I'd like to go downstairs for dinner, but I looked down at my dress. It was dirty and stained, and all the girls here looked so nice. How could I go down, dressed in these rags? Then I remembered the donations.

I jumped up and looked around for a staff member. Louise Thomas came out of her door. She and Joe and their little boy, Junior, had a room right next to the kicking room.

"Mrs. Benton told me I could get some clothes," I said. "Where do I go to get them?"

"Mrs. Benton's in charge of the blessing room," she said. "Just a second, and I'll take you up."

"Blessing room? What's that?" I asked as we climbed the stairs to the Benton's apartment.

Louise chuckled. "That's where the donated clothing is kept. You know, 'Blessings and Son.' "

I didn't know, but I kept my mouth shut and followed her. While we waited for Mrs. Benton, Louise introduced me to the three Benton children, Marji, Connie and Jim.

I remembered Connie—she'd come into the kicking room and told me, "Remember I'll be praying for you." She was only thirteen, too. Marji was a pretty teen-ager of sixteen. She told me how glad she was I was there. Jim was ten. He stuck out his hand and shook mine vigorously. Such well-behaved youngsters, and so natural!

"Hi, Carmen." It was Mrs. Benton. "You must be feeling better. Louise says you want some clothes."

"I sure could use some," I said rather ruefully, and gestured at the blouse and skirt I was wearing.

"Guess you could. Come on and we'll see what we can find. What size do you wear?"

"A seven, I think. . . ." I really didn't know, I hadn't

bought any clothes in ages. I just threw on whatever was there. I knew I'd lost a lot of weight, but I really didn't know my size.

We walked up to the third floor. Mrs. Benton pointed out Janet's room, and Susan's. Susan was just coming out, and Mrs. Benton introduced us.

"You must be the new girl Eileen was telling me about," Susan said cheerfully. "We're all glad you came, and I know the Lord is going to help you."

"Susan is in charge of our Family Pac Program," Mrs. Benton said. "She's a great salesman, and the girls help her. All of them enjoy it; maybe someday you may help her out."

"You just keep looking up, and the Lord will do the rest," Susan said, and she headed downstairs.

Mrs. Benton and I walked down the hall to the blessing room, which held two long racks of dresses and coats. Boxes and cartons of all sizes were stacked against the walls.

"Wish *I* could wear a size seven," Mrs. Benton said, as she started to examine the dresses on the rack. "Here's one. Like red and white?"

I was relieved when I saw the dress. I'd been a little leery about the *donation* bit and hoped they wouldn't be too ragged looking. These dresses looked new.

"Isn't it a little long?" I asked. I'd been used to mini-minis on the street.

Mrs. Benton looked at me, as though measuring me. "Not too," she said. "It looks about right. We don't wear them any shorter than two inches above the knee here."

She handed me three more dresses, a couple of blouses and skirts and some underwear. She gestured toward a shelf that had kits of toothbrushes, toothpaste, deodorants, and so on. "Help yourself," she said, and went on looking over things.

I went out of there laden down. "Gee, thanks a lot," I said.

"Don't thank me. Thank the Lord."

"Well, thank the Lord," I said. It sounded strange, but I meant it sincerely.

I spread the stuff all out on my bed in the kicking room and examined it greedily. Then I looked at the clock and realized I didn't have much time to gloat if I was to be ready for supper. I raced into the shower, dressed carefully, arranged my hair over my scars and made my entrance.

Everyone complimented me on my appearance. Everyone went out of his way to be pleasant. It was a wonderful feeling. I slept like a baby that night—eight full hours.

The next day I decided to go to chapel. I was still pretty weak, but I managed and I enjoyed it. Mr. Downes, the caretaker, spoke about "the goodness of the Lord." As I listened to him, I began to realize that this beautiful home, this staff —even the clothes I had on and the food I ate—was Christ's expression of His love for us.

I went back and lay down afterwards, but I couldn't go to sleep. Again, I tossed and turned. Then I remembered Barb. She'd said to meet her today; maybe a cigarette would help.

I knew she was at Bible Class, so I posted myself at the door to catch her. As soon as I spotted her, I rushed up, and said, "Hi, what about a cigarette?"

Barb looked around nervously. "Didn't you hear what happened? Eileen had me on the carpet for smoking. I gave her my last cigarettes, and she put me on probation."

"You're a fool," I said. "Why didn't you just give her one cigarette? Why'd you give her all of them?"

Barb gave me a steady look. "I want to stay, Carmen. That's why. Eileen and I prayed together and she told me if I had the craving again to come to her and we'd pray again. I've been praying most of the day, and it's helped. I'm on my way to the basement to pray now. I really do want to stop. Want to join me?"

I shook my head. I needed a cigarette, not prayer.

Lunch saved my nerves. Mrs. Downes really was a good cook. But afterwards I had nothing to do. I decided to go down by the pool. I sat a while on the bank and watched Jim and his friends cavorting in the water.

Then a voice came out of the blue, "Hey, you can't smoke here!"

I looked up guiltily. I wanted one so bad, I was sure someone knew. Then I tracked down the voice. A girl—Eleanor—up by the diving board, was yelling at a kid down by the bridge.

"I'll get it from him," I yelled, and took off for the bridge. The poor little boy didn't know what hit him. I yanked the cigarette from his lips, muttered, "Get outta here, before you get into more trouble," and ran behind the bushes and inhaled. I smoked the cigarette greedily, almost burning my fingers off.

Then I went back to the kicking room, and fell fast asleep. I woke up just in time for supper and ate an enormous meal. I was feeling fine, until Eileen asked me to come into her office.

I followed her, but all the while I was trying to figure out why? I was suspicious.

"Carmen, why were you smoking down by the pool?" she asked.

"Me? You're crazy. I wasn't smoking."

We sat in silence for a few minutes, then Eileen spoke again.

"It doesn't really make that much difference to me whether you've smoked or not. What does matter is that we try to teach our girls honesty. This is one of the first lessons you must learn here."

I stared at her. How did she know? Had Eleanor told her?

"I wasn't smoking," I said again. "You want me to leave?"

"Please, be honest, Carmen," Eileen pleaded.

My mind was churning. Obviously she knew. I stared at her, defiantly. She looked right back at me.

"OK. I did have a drag this afternoon."

"Do you have any cigarettes left?"

"No."

"Carmen, I want to help you. If you have any cigarettes left, get rid of them. That way you won't be tempted."

"I don't have any," I said stubbornly. And that wasn't any lie. I wished I had.

"Are you sure they're all gone?" Eileen asked.

"Yeah, man. I told you they were all gone, didn't I?" I was beginning to get mad.

"Just a minute," Eileen said politely. "We don't use that expression 'Yeah, man,' here. We call that street language."

"Honest, I don't have any, Eileen. I'm sorry. I won't do it again. You can search me if you want to."

"It's not necessary for me to search you, Carmen. All I want you to do is not smoke again. We are not here to condemn you, but to help you get rid of all your bad habits."

"OK," I said, and got up to go. "I won't do it again."

"Good." Eileen smiled. "Let me pray with you before you go, so Christ can help you."

She asked Christ to make me honest; she asked him to take away my smoking habit and replace it with the Bible habit.

It all sounded sensible, I thought, as I walked away, but it was just too unreal. Why were these people praying for me? They didn't even know me.

The following day I started classes. It was hard to concentrate. It was a long time since I'd been in school. Joe's classes were good because he drew diagrams of everything. By the time I got to the Reverend Benton's class on "Successful Motivation," I was able to concentrate, and I listened intently. Motivation was something I really needed if I was to start a new life.

The following Sunday I attended church. It reminded me of the times I went with Cathy and her parents. The worship was interesting and inspiring and the people were friendly.

That afternoon I moved out of the kicking room into a lovely double room. Ellie was my roommate. She wasn't a drug addict, but she was a chronic runaway from home. She claimed to be a Christian and pestered me constantly about my sinful ways but, as the days wore on, sometimes I wondered. We got along all right, on the whole, but once in a while she'd flare up and accuse me of some outlandish thing.

One day she yelled that I was taking the Benton children away from her. "They're *my* friends, not yours," she ended.

"What do you mean *your* friends? Those kids are like little brothers and sisters to me. I never had any of my own.

I love being with them; they're such nice children. Besides, they are the ones who ask me to play games and ride with them. They're nice to all the girls."

But Ellie insisted I was trying to cut her out. She got madder and madder, and finally threatened to clobber me with a chair.

I could feel my own temperature rising. "Listen, sister," I said, as calmly as I could, "you claim to be a Christian, and you're always rapping about my sinful life. Well, you're no saint, yourself."

"Oh, shut up," Ellie snarled and took hold of the back of the chair.

I jumped up, my fists clenched. No little whippersnapper was going to get away with telling me to shut up. I was ready to let her have it, then something within me held me back. What it was, I don't know, but I put my arm down, drew a deep breath and walked out.

I bumped into Sally. I knew she must have heard us yelling and she was bound to notice the expression on my face.

"What's the matter? You look as though you'd been run over by a truck."

"Oh, nothing," I mumbled.

"What really did happen?" she persisted as we walked on down the hall.

"Oh, that Ellie can really bug me!"

"Come on into my room and tell me about it."

I followed Sally to her room and spilled the whole story. She seemed to understand.

"You've got to understand, Carmen," she said. "Ellie has emotional problems. She's not crazy or anything like that, but she does have a mixed-up personality."

"She sure does! I was going to let her have it, but something stopped me and I decided it wasn't worth it."

"It's a good thing you didn't. We don't allow any fighting. If you'd started, you'd have been dismissed immediately."

"But what can I do? I can't just go back and say nothing."

"Why don't you apoligize to Ellie?"

I looked at Sally in amazement. "*Me* apologize? What for? I didn't do anything."

"I know that," Sally said patiently. "You are not sorry because of her accusations; you're sorry because your relationship with her turned out so badly. You can apologize for that, can't you? For the misunderstanding? Not for taking Connie, Jim and Marji away from her."

"Well, I don't know," I said doubtfully.

"Try it," she urged. "I'm sure it will work out. The Bible says to turn the other cheek, love your enemies. You do it and I know you'll be amazed at how *your* attitude will change *her* attitude."

"OK, I'll try it. I hope it works."

Ellie was sitting on the bed staring at the floor when I walked in. I was still awfully mad at her, but I had promised, so I ploughed in.

"Ellie," I blurted out, "I'm sorry about what happened. I don't want to get mad at you and I don't want you to get mad at me. Will you please forgive me?"

I tried to sound sincere, but I knew it sounded corny—she'd never believe me.

Ellie jumped up from the bed. "Oh, Carmen," she cried, "it was all my fault. I had no right to accuse you. I guess you're right; my Christianity is weak. Will you forgive me?"

Well, well, I thought, so there are other ways of disarming a person besides with a knife or razor. This way was certainly easier, and it kept you out of jail.

Later, I told Sally that Ellie and I had made up and she didn't sound surprised. The whole episode made me think a lot. I still hadn't experienced the feeling I'd had when I'd been with Cathy. I didn't really know if I wanted to be a Christian; I'd have to give up so much.

On day Mrs. Benton invited me to ride along to the bakery with her. On the way in, she told me that the owner gave us day-old bread and pastries for free. She said he was a wonderful man who'd had a great tragedy: his teen-age daughter had been killed in an automobile accident. She told me he helped us out, she thought, by sharing with us what God had given him, and he liked to do it for the girls in the Home.

Then she changed the subject, and asked, "How are things going for you, Carmen?"

"I guess all right," I said slowly, "but it seems awfully hard to be a Christian."

"Have you surrendered your life to Christ yet?"

"Not really."

"Until you're on the Lord's side, you have to fight your battles alone. Once you give your life to Christ, He gives you strength and grace to meet your problems. 'I can do all things through Christ which strengtheneth me.' That's Philippians 4:13. Believe me, it's much harder to serve the devil. Look what he's done to *your* life; you've walked the streets, you've been a junkie and you've gone to jail. But Jesus said, 'I am come that they may have life, and that they might have it more abundantly' (John 10:10). And He really does want to do that for you," she concluded.

What she said made sense, I knew. We rode in silence

for a long time, while I mulled over her words. She and the staff all had *something*—whatever it was, I wanted it. Was it really Jesus?

On the ride back, Mrs. Benton kept encouraging me to surrender my life to Christ. I didn't argue with her; a battle was raging within me. I would either have to give my life to Christ or I would have to leave the home. Somehow I had to decide, and soon.

Then, one day, Christ did become real to me. I was talking to one of the girls and I came right out and asked her how she had received Christ. She said it was simple. Just ask Christ to forgive you your sins, receive Him into you heart by faith and then live for Him.

Just one, two, three. It sounded easy, but for me it was hard. I wandered down by the bridge alone, staying away from the small bridge. I'd stopped smoking and I didn't want to be reminded of it. I slumped down on the grass by the falls and repeated what I'd just heard: Ask Christ to forgive you your sins.

"Either I give my life to Christ, or I . . . ," I said aloud.

I looked up and then I began to pray—hesitantly at first.

"Jesus, forgive me as a sinner. I'm sorry for what I've done. Help me to be a different person; help me to forget drugs. Change my life. Help me now and come into my heart. In Jesus' name. Amen."

I felt something flowing into me, something natural and sweet and strong.

"Jesus," I cried out, "take control of my life. Lord, help me to live again."

I had a feeling of peace. "Jesus, you're real," I whispered. I felt it way down in my heart—Jesus *was* real!

I ran all the way back to the house. I had to tell everyone what I'd experienced. I told the glad news to some girls standing on the porch and then raced into the house to tell the whole staff. Brother Benton was reading the paper and he looked up, as I announced dramatically, "Christ has just come into my heart!"

"Well, praise the Lord," he said. "Isn't the Lord good?"

That night I went to hear Arthur James speak. Arthur and his wife, Karen, represented our home in other churches. They were invited to speak at churches all over the land, and the Reverend Benton often said that if it weren't for Arthur and Karen, we'd never be able to pay our bills.

Just before he spoke, Eileen asked me to give my testimony. I was scared, standing before all the girls, but I gulped and said that until now Christ had lived outside my heart, but now He was the King of my life and He was living within me. I said He gave me the strength to give up drugs and to always live for Him. I had tears in my eyes when I finished and most of my audience did too.

But I still had a lot to learn. Living for Christ takes a total commitment, even in small things. One day, I skimped on the dusting I was supposed to do. Eileen checked me out and told me I'd have to do an extra hour's work on Saturday.

"I hate work," I lashed out at her. "I wish I never had to do any." I guess my life as a Christian had not yet flowed over into the work program.

"Carmen, we could hire someone to do the work, but that isn't for the best. We don't expect you girls to be slaves; we work along with you, don't we? But working teaches discipline and discipline builds holiness and holiness builds character."

"How is an extra hour on Saturday going to make me holier?" I asked, hoping to trap her.

But Eileen just smiled, and said, "That extra hour will remind you that discipline builds holiness; holiness builds character."

Gradually, I came to love the whole staff. Their personalities were very different, but each one seemed to have a real concern for each of us girls. Each one of the staff poured out love and concern for us. I just couldn't figure out why they loved us. *I* certainly had nothing to give them back.

One night, I couldn't sleep. I got up and wandered down the hall, hoping to find someone to talk to. I went past the kicking room and looked in. Sally was there, rubbing a girl's back. Why? I wondered. Why was Sally giving up a night's sleep to help a girl who was kicking?

Sally was also checking lights out that night and when she stuck her head in the door, I whispered, "Got a minute?"

"Sure," she said and came over and sat on the edge of my bed.

"Sally, that girl who's kicking—do you really love her?"

"Why, of course,"

"But why?"

"To show her the love of Christ."

"What do you mean by that?"

"No one likes to see a girl go through the suffering and pain of withdrawal. Rubbing that girl's back gives me a chance to show her that I love her. Staying up with her, rubbing her back, cleaning up—all these show her the love of Christ."

"Sally, you're a saint," I said and lay back on my pillow.

She laughed as she got up, patted my cheek and said, "And you'd make a good angel."

As time went on I learned to put Christ first in my life. Occasionally I had my hangups, but I learned the secret of praying through them. When I talked to God about my difficulties, they seemed to get solved. My problems remained the same, but I was changing. It was more than worth it.

One day I told Mrs. Benton I wanted to live for Christ more than anything else.

She looked at me carefully, then said, "Carmen you need the baptism of the Holy Spirit. Tonight at the prayer meeting I will pray with you, so you can receive the baptism."

I was, of course, familiar with the baptism of the Holy Spirit; I had read of it in the Book of Acts many times, and Janet had explained it to me once before.,

That evening after a short talk by Joe, we got down on our knees to pray. Mrs. Benton was beside me.

"Don't seek baptism," she told me, "seek the Baptizer, Christ. Praise the Lord and worship Him, love Jesus in your heart, then ask the Lord to baptize you with his Holy Spirit."

I lifted my hands and began to praise the Lord. I thanked Him for all that He had done for me, and for changing my life so dramatically.

Mrs. Benton laid her hands on me and began to pray. As she prayed, I asked Jesus to baptize me with the Holy Spirit. The rest of the girls saw what was happening, and came over to pray with me. Then it happened. It's most difficult to explain, but after I received the baptism of the Holy Spirit, my Christian life took on a new dimension.

My year's stay at the Home was nearing its end. The staff had encouraged me to go on to Bible School at Rhinebeck so I could learn more of God's word. It was hard for me to leave.

The last night the staff held a banquet for five of us who were graduating from the program. Each of us told of our experiences before we came to the Home and of the change in our lives.

It had been difficult for me to come here; now it was difficult to leave. I had found a real home here, real people who loved me, and, best of all, a real Jesus. I didn't want to leave.

But I did, and at Rhinebeck, there was Vinnie. He'd kept in touch with me, while I was in Garrison, but now we started to see a lot of each other. We were wary at first, but as time went on, it seemed that God had put love for each other into our hearts.

Our courtship was serious—and funny. Although the other students knew that Vinnie and I had lived together for years, they treated us like a newly met couple, who had fallen in love and wanted to get married.

At the end of my first year of Bible School, the Reverend Benton performed the ceremony, and all of the staff from the Home and the girls were there. I was so proud of my new husband, I almost burst. Next to receiving Christ as my Saviour and Baptizer, my marriage to Vinnie is the greatest thing that ever happened to me!

We live in Ohio now, Vinnie was invited to become Assistant Pastor at a church there, after his graduation. *And*—one other important event—the Lord has blessed our home with a baby boy. His name? John, naturally.

Praise the Lord!

Epilogue

As you've read my story, maybe you've realized that you need to receive Jesus as your Savior. Or maybe you are away from God and need to get back. You could be reading about me in a prison cell. Or maybe you're reading in bed. Or sitting down. Wherever you are, why don't you slip to your knees and ask Jesus to forgive your sins and come into your heart? His still small voice will speak to your heart as it did to mine. If you ask Him to forgive you your sins and if you accept Him as your Savior, He will give you a wonderful, glorious future. I know He will.

I am praying for you. I hope you learn to walk with Jesus through life. He wants to walk with you—as He does with me!

Glossary

acid—LSD (Lysergic acid diethylamide)

busted—arrested

carrier—transporter of drugs

cold turkey—sudden withdrawal from drugs, with no medication

connection—drugseller

cop—to buy drugs

cooker—bottle cap used to heat heroin and water solution

dolly—dolophine (methadone)

drill—to inject drugs with a needle

flip out—to lose physical, mental, and emotional control after taking drugs

fix—an injection of drugs

freak out—same as flip out

gay—homosexual (emotion or feelings for persons of same sex)

get off—to take an injection of drugs

heterosexuality—feeling toward persons of the opposite sex

high—to be under the influence of drugs

hit—same as get off

hustle—to prostitute

junk—narcotic

junkie—a narcotics addict

kicking—going through the process of withdrawing from drugs

Lesbian—a female homosexual

mainline—to take drugs intravenously

OD—overdose of drugs, often lethal

Old Man—protector, pimp, or roommate of prostitute

pimp—a man who solicits customers for the prostitute and shares in the proceeds

pot—marijuana

pros—prostitution

pusher—seller of drugs

score—to obtain drugs

shoot—to take drugs by needle

skin pop—to inject drugs under the skin

smack—heroin

snort—to take drugs by sniffing through the nose

stick—marijuana

stuff—a loose term for any drug.

trick—a prostitute's pickup

tracks—marks left from the injection of needles

trip—hallucinogenic experience, usually involving LSD

turned on—excited about something, usually from drugs

turned off—lost interest

weed—marijuana

works—instruments used for taking drugs: cooker, syringe.